I

"I'm telling you, I don't want to be a part of this anymore," the woman cried, following the man from her bathroom to her bedroom. "It's getting to be too much. Too many people are involved, which means someone's going to find out."

"No one will find out if you keep your mouth shut."

"But that's just it," she protested. "My husband's breathing down my neck wanting to know what I'm keeping from him, you-know-who is out of control as usual-"

"Maybe you should've thought of that before you started sleeping with him."

She put her hands on her hips. "Maybe I should've thought of this before I started sleeping with you."

He grabbed her roughly by the shoulders. "You're no innocent victim, so quit acting like it. You wanted this, remember? You were tired of your stuffy marriage and your boring life. So suck it up. We're in this-all of us-until the end. So get used to it." He shoved her down on the bed.

She tried to get away but he grabbed her, pinning her down. Her heart was beating wildly and part of her loathed him but she couldn't help it; she gave in and kissed him. He kissed her back, roughly at first as he always did but then slightly softer, just the way she liked it.

Later that night she was alone-her husband was working late again-and decided to try and get some sleep. With everything weighing on her, however, she knew it wouldn't be an easy task.

Why did I do this? she wondered as she stared up at the ceiling, pulling her silk sheets more tightly around her. *Was my life really that boring that I had to let things get this far?*

Suddenly she heard movement downstairs. She wasn't alarmed at first; it was probably just the cat. But then she heard the unmistakable sound of footsteps, heavy footsteps which could only mean one thing: her husband was home.

She quickly closed her eyes and rolled over to one side, pretending to be asleep. Silence followed until she felt pressure on the other side of the bed, where he had obviously sat down next to her.

Then he grabbed her arm and her eyes popped wide open as she stared into the face of the man who definitely wasn't her husband. "What are you doing here?" she asked softly. "I thought we weren't going to meet until-"

Suddenly he moved his hands toward her neck, applying pressure. It happened so quickly, before she could even cry out. She noticed then that he was wearing black gloves and it quickly sank in what he was happening.

He was going to kill her.

She fought back with all her might, thrashing and kicking furiously. She tried to scratch him but all she could reach were his gloves and didn't make a dent.

She started choking then, gasping for breath that wasn't coming. She did everything in her power to fight, to survive, but her strength was waning and she knew in the depths of her soul that she wasn't going to survive this.

A feeling of calm passed over her body and she could feel it growing more still. At last it gave a final jerk and she saw nothing but darkness.

Chapter One

SIX MONTHS LATER

Darrell knew he was being followed.

It wasn't something he could be absolutely sure of at first; it was just a feeling, a strong feeling that caused perspiration to snake down his neck and drip under his shirt collar. It probably didn't help that he knew vital information that could bury powerful city officials. He was sitting on a ticking time-bomb, with no warning of when-or how-it would go off.

I'm quitting my job, he thought as he quickened his pace. *Get Lisa, move to some tropical island and forget this nightmare ever happened.* It wasn't about wanting a career change; it was about survival. He wanted to live to see his thirtieth birthday.

After what seemed like hours he made it across the deserted parking garage to his car. By that time he's managed to calm down, feeling his thoughts weren't completely justified. *Just because I know what I know doesn't mean anyone else does. I'm just panicking. The best thing to do now is relax.* Shaking his head at his tendency to see the worst in every situation he hit the button on the keyless entry pad.

In that split second he knew something was wrong.

He didn't have time to react, however. As soon as he hit the button a deafening explosion shook the parking garage, incinerating everything within a five-mile radius.

***

Dex Angelo knew time was running out.

The whole thing had beyond spun out of control. First her, then the computer analyst…and now Dex was sitting in a deserted bar in Costa Rica, wondering what his next move should be.

I should go back, he thought as he stared into his empty glass. *There's nothing left…except the money. Always comes back down to the money. A fat lot of good it'll do now.*

But if he went back he was a dead man and he knew it; it'd all be over. With all the loose ends involved…he'd never be free.

You call this free? the other side of him argued. *You might as well be in prison. This is eating you alive.* And it was. Never in his life did Dex think he could sink so low.

So it was simple. He had to go back. It wouldn't fix anything, but it was the right thing to do.

Wasn't it?

***

"…and police still have no leads in the murder of local computer consultant Darrell Emery, who car exploded two weeks ago today in the parking garage ofNabor Electronics and Development, Mr. Emery's employer. If anyone had any information pertaining to this case they
are encouraged to come forward…"

"Would you turn that down?" Rosanna Howard called from her desk, trying to concentrate on her work. It was difficult, however, when the other employees wanted to watch the news and listen to the story of grisly murder that happened only a few blocks away from Taylor Publishing, where Rosanna worked as an editor.

She'd been with Taylor for four years, hired two years after she graduated from college. It was a job she truly enjoyed, and she enjoyed the people she worked with. It was just that every now and then they could get preoccupied...like they were right now.

"Sorry, Rosanna," Amy Price said sheepishly as she walked by. "We couldn't help but listen, since it happened so close to here and all-"

Rosanna groaned inwardly. "It's alright, Amy," she said to the eager-to-please recently hired twenty-three-year-old who looked like she was twelve.

Rosanna knew she was intimidating to some of the younger hires. She didn't try to be but she was a tough, no-nonsense type of worker that expected things to be done quickly and efficiently. Still, all in all she could complain about the environment she worked in.

Right now she was currently editing what she hoped would be a best-seller if she could
just get the wording and formatting right. Wayne Aames was a promising young writer, and she was happy to get the chance to work with him.

Later in the afternoon she was approached by Jason Graham, an editor who'd been there longer than she. "Hey Rose," he greeted her. "A few of us are going out for drinks after we get out of here. Want to come?"

Rosanna gritted her teeth; only Nora was allowed to call her "Rose" and everyone knew that. Still, it didn't stop people from trying, especially Jason or people wanting to annoy her. She was used to his friendly attempts to get her to go out with him and their other co-workers, which she always politely refused; she had her own friends at work at Jason was only after her because he wanted to go out with her. He was nice enough but too arrogant for Rosanna's tastes.

"I can't tonight," she told him, not looking up from her computer screen.

"You always say that. What is it this time? You have to work late again?"

"Actually, I have plans," she told him, knowing that would get the message across. And, as it turned out, it wasn't a lie.

Jason didn't hide his disappointment as he walked away and Rosanna felt a slight twinge of guilt. It faded as she continued to work and was visited by her friends, Gayle and Lucy, who had the latest gossip to report.

Rosanna was one of the last to leave that evening, which wasn't unusual, and she went down to the parking garage somewhat hesitantly. After what happened to that guy on the news being alone in a parking garage at night would make anyone leery, even someone as put-together and focused as herself.

As she sat in her traffic she tried to call her sister one more time but it went straight to voicemail, again, which led Rosanna to believe she had it turned off, which wasn't unusual these days. After Nora's messy divorce she seldom felt like talking to anyone but her sister, which was why Rosanna suggested they go out tonight. It would boost Nora's spirits to indulge on Italian food, rich dessert, and good wine. Help her start to forget how Eric Frost treated her.

She was in a gridlock, which reminded Rosanna of how much she hated driving in New York. She only did it because she liked to be independent but sometimes it really got to her.

She was finally starting to move again when her engine suddenly coughed and sputtered before completely stalling out. *Come on,* Rosanna silently begged as she tried to restart the car. *Not now…*

After her car had been towed to the nearest garage Rosanna followed in a cab and finally reached her sister, telling her why she'd be a little late. When she arrived at the garage she was told she needed a specific part, that could be found at Mason Auto, which wasn't too far away. Opting to walk, Rosanna left, her heels clicking on the concrete as she maneuvered around the other travelers.

When she arrived at Mason Auto she saw that it was quite busy, and the line wrapped around the first aisle. Sighing impatiently, she took her place at the back and began the long process of waiting.

It was finally her turn to be helped and Rosanna waited while the salesman went in back to get her car part. The front door jangled, causing her to reflexively turn around but she couldn't see who walked in. Then the salesman came back with her part. "Here you are, ma'am."

Rosanna produced her credit card and made the purchase, thanking the salesman before turning to go. She headed toward the door and paused, searching her bag for her phone to let Nora know she was on her way. Distracted by rummaging through it as she walked, she collided with someone rounding the corner of an aisle. "I'm sorry," she began, readjusting her purse on her shoulder. "Are you alright?"

"Maybe you should watch where you're going next time, Rose."

Rosanna's head shot up, her eyes focusing on the man belonging to the irritating voice she knew so well. He was wearing a C. and Sons' Construction hoodie and looking at her with a mixture of amusement and disdain. She let out a long breath, shaking her head. "Jess Coleman."

***

Nora Howard looked at her watch for the third time, seeing it was only five minutes later than the last time she checked. Rosanna was known for running late because of work but tonight she actually had an excuse that Nora could understand: her car broke down. Still, Nora would've been perfectly happy to sit at home with a Salisbury steak frozen dinner watching old sitcoms. Instead she was at a ridiculously priced restaurant getting stares of pity from people who obviously thought her date had stood her up.

Would it be better if they knew the truth? Nora thought bitterly as she sipped her wine. *That I'm an over-thirty divorcee waiting for my little sister to "cheer me up"?* She shook her head slightly, causing her long, light brown hair to swing from side to side. She felt unbearably pathetic.

Her thoughts turned to Eric then, about everything that had happened and she squeezed her eyes shut, trying to get the image of their wedding day out of her mind. Then she remembered her sister, knowing she would come in at any moment to distract her, which she excelled at.

At least one good thing came out of this divorce for someone, Nora told herself. Though Nora didn't agree, Rosanna thought Eric's younger brother was the scum of the earth. *At least she won't have to worry about being related to him anymore. In fact, I'll be surprised if they ever have to see one another ever again.*

***

Jess took a step toward her, his dark-blonde hair gleaming in the overhead light. "What's got you so distracted?" he wanted to know, deliberately blocking her path to the door.

"Dinner," she answered shortly, trying to maneuver her way around him.

"Who's the poor sap?" he prodded, obviously finding her attempts to thwart him amusing.

"It's not a 'he', it's a 'she'," Rosanna snapped.

Jess raised an eyebrow. "Really?"

"Oh shut up." Rosanna finally pushed her way past him, beginning to walk down the sidewalk. She felt her irritation grow when the door jangled behind her, footsteps following momentarily. "Don't you have something to buy?" she asked in annoyance. "Or someone?"

"You know I never have to pay." Jess fell into step beside her. "And it's been so long since I've seen you I figured why not start up a friendly chat."

Rosanna glared at him. "I'm in a hurry, okay? Go bother a dog or something."

"I saw my brother today at work," he said, stopping behind her.

Rosanna paused, slowly turning around. "Is that why you won't leave me alone? You're here to plead his case yet again?"

"He's really sorry, Rose."

"Don't call me that," she snapped.

"Fine. He's really sorry *Rosanna*."

She shook her head in disbelief. "Sorry?" she repeated incredulously. "Do you know I'm meeting for dinner tonight? My sister. Remember my sweet, dedicated, devoted sister who did nothing but try and make your crappy excuse of a half-brother happy? And how does he repay her?"

"Rosanna-"

"He has an affair," she finished, undaunted. "With a high school student."

"At least she was legal," Jess pointed out. "Otherwise he'd be really sick."

Disgust overcoming her, Rosanna began to back away. "I won't even dignify that with a comment of any kind." She paused.

"He shouldn't send you to do his dirty work. And it doesn't matter anymore anyway. They're divorced. It's over. Nora can finally move on with her life."

"He screwed up. Big time," he added hastily when he saw Rosanna raise an eyebrow. "He knows what he did was wrong. Can't she at least hear him out?"

Rosanna whirled on him. "What is this? Are you trying to live vicariously through Eric or some crap? He's a grown man; he can fight his own battles. His other battles anyway. But this? This is a dead issue. My sister's finally free of him. Tell him I said to go to hell."

Jess chuckled softly. "You're a real self-righteous bitch, aren't you?"

"And you're a dick," Rosanna shot back. "Another bonus to this divorce is no longer being legally related to you. Go buy yourself some entertainment for the night and leave me the hell alone." She shoved past him and stalked off.

"Do you have any idea where we are?" Jess asked suddenly.

Rosanna looked around, finally acknowledging her surroundings. So wrapped up in her firery conversation with Jess she hadn't noticed they'd walked far off the sidewalk and into a deserted alleyway behind a strip of what seemed to be abandoned buildings.

"Great," she muttered. "I'm far from cabs, I can't find my phone, and I'm over an hour late meeting Nora."

"You should've paid more attention while you were being so utterly charming." His voice dripped with sarcasm.

"You could have too," she shot back. "This is all your fault anyway. Make yourself useful and let me borrow your phone."

"You're kidding, right?"

"Now!" she barked, holding out her palm.

"I can't refuse a bossy woman." He handed her his phone.

"No service." Rosanna gave Jess his phone. Then she resumed stalking away.

"Wait!" Jess grabbed her by the shoulder. "Don't go that way."

"Which way then?" The alley had four turn-offs.

Jess nodded straight ahead. "Let's try that one."

They walked down the turn-off and discovered it was a dead-end. Wordlessly, they tried the next one over.

Rosanna rounded the corner first and saw something that made her stop cold. A group of men were standing next to the dumpster yards away, their backs turned to her. They were shouting and arguing and one man had a gun pulled on another, who was kneeling.

As if that weren't enough to make her heart race there was something else she noticed: these weren't ordinary men. They were wearing NYPD uniforms except the man with the gun, who was standing in such a way his detective badge was exposed.

Cops, Rosanna managed to think frantically as the scene unfolded in front of her. *They're cops.*

Chapter Two

The detective had his gun directly pointed at the head of the kneeling man, who was pleading over and over again for mercy. "I'll never tell," he kept saying. "No one will ever know I'm the one that put the bomb in Emery's car."

Rosanna was frozen where she stood, unable to think clearly or react. She barely felt it when Jess bumped her from behind, immediately stiffening. Rosanna instinctively grabbed his hand and he began to pull her backward.

"You're right," the detective agreed. "No one will ever know."

A deafening shot rang out, echoing down the alleyway. Rosanna opened her mouth to scream but Jess clamped a hand over it firmly, urging her backward.

This can't be happening, Rosanna thought, panicking. *There's no possible way we just saw what we saw. This is real life, not a movie-*

Jess's grip intensified and Rosanna realized her legs weren't moving. The look in his eyes reflected her own terror and confusion and she realized that no matter how she felt she had to move so they could get out of there.

As they carefully inched their way backward a cry suddenly rang out. "Hey!" a voice shouted, outraged. One of the uniformed police officers pointed to them, causing frenzied shouting from the others.

"Come on!" Jess yelled, pulling on her frantically. "Move, dammit!"

Rosanna snapped out of her stupor, allowing Jess to keep pulling on her. Turning to go, she saw guns being raised out of the corner of her eye. Screaming as shots were fired, she broke into a run.

"This way!" Jess shouted, still grasping her hand. They ran together, managing to escape the alley.

"What now?" Rosanna demanded as they ran across the busy highway, looking over her shoulder as they dodged traffic. Their pursuers weren't far behind.

Jess came to a stop, looking over the guardrail and into the water below. Then he looked at Rosanna. "We jump."

Rosanna looked at him incredulously. "We what?"

"We do it now, we just might survive this." He was already climbing over.

Rosanna sputtered in protest. "Jess, this is the Brooklyn Bridge. We can't just jump."

"We have to. It's the only way to throw them off our trail. Come on, it won't be that bad."

She shook her head vehemently. "No way. There's no way-" She broke off suddenly. "Jess," she said, her tone abruptly changing.

His back was still turned. "Just because the shooting stopped doesn't mean we're in the clear. We can do it, Rose. Come on."

"Jess," Rosanna said again, her voice sick with fear.

"We don't have time to argue!" Jess snapped impatiently. "Quit being so stubborn for once in your life and just trust me." He held his hand out.

"I can't."

"Why not?"

"Because there's a gun barrel being jabbed into my back."

Jess stopped, slowly turning around. He saw the uniformed cops who now formed a semi-circle around them, preventing any escape. The detective was standing behind Rosanna, watching Jess in mild amusement. "Where you off to son? The current's pretty strong this time of year."

"Thought I'd take a swim, for the hell of it. You know us young people, always thrill-seeking." He nodded to Rosanna. "That's what my girlfriend and I were up to tonight so if you could just let us get back to it. We're not hurting anybody." He kept his tone light, his eyes never leaving Rosanna's terrified expression.

"I'm afraid I can't do that." He tightened his grip on Rosanna, causing her breath to catch. "We need to talk about what you and your girl, here, saw tonight."

"Nothing," Jess said quickly. "We didn't see anything-"

"We saw you," Rosanna interrupted, "cornering a criminal. Doing your job." She threw Jess a desperate look.

"She's right," Jess said on cue, impressed with her quick thinking. "We'll swear to it, if we have to."

The detective considered this. "Alright," he said at last, releasing Rosanna who promptly fled to Jess. "This is what we're going to do."

Jess discreetly reached for Rosanna's hand and quickly caught her eye. Dread rising in her throat, Rosanna knew what he wanted to do. What had to be done.

They carefully inched backward until they could climb over the rail. Jess counted to three under his breath and they turned around, taking the plunge.

Rosanna was dimly aware of the shots being fired as they hurtled over the ledge and toward the flowing water far below. She didn't even have time to scream.

As if it were alive, reaching out with long, curled fingers, the water latched onto Rosanna, pulling her deep into the depths below, its grip viselike. Kicking desperately against the tug of the current, she fought as hard as she could to break the surface.

Breathing in deep gulps of air greedily Jess surfaced, trying to get his bearings. Squinting in the darkness he realized the only sound he could hear was the rushing water. *No gunshots,* he thought in satisfaction. *They must think we're dead.* It was then he realized he was alone.

"Rosanna?" he called uncertainly, his voice barely carrying over the noisy water. "Rosanna!" he called again, louder this time. Swimming with the current he looked frantically around for any sign of her.

There was none.

Refusing to give up so quickly, he took a deep breath and went underwater, feeling around blindly in the darkness.

At last his hand brushed against something and he grabbed on, yanking her up with all his might.

Gasping for air he looked down at Rosanna's still form, then desperately around for any kind of relief.

He found it not too far off: a rocky bank stood out against all the water a few yards away. Feeling more grateful than he could ever remember feeling before, Jess let the current pull them along until they got closer, then he swam with all his might until he reached it.

Dragging Rosanna onto the uneven ground he stayed on his knees for a moment, waiting for a moment for his breathing to return to normal. Then he approached her, appalled by her still unmoving body and pallor.

Relief flooded him when he found a pulse. Scrambling to recall what little he knew about CPR, he began chest compressions, pausing long enough to breathe for her.

"Dammit Rose," he muttered as he continued to work on her. "You really are a stubborn piece of work, you know that? You have been ever since I've known you. Use that now. Breathe."

He kept working but she remained still, and the reality began to hit him that she might not recover. Refusing to let his mind wander there he kept going.

Suddenly he saw her chest heave and he stopped. Coughing violently, Rosanna turned to the side, choking on water and gasping for air. Jess felt the tension leave his body, looking up at the sky in a moment of silent thanks.

Her heart pounding, Rosanna's eyes slowly looked upward, trying to focus on Jess's concerned face. She immediately grabbed his hand, squeezing tightly as she continued to gasp for air.

They just stayed there that way for a long moment before Jess finally spoke. "It's okay," he told her quietly. "You're gonna be fine. Just keep breathing."

Rosanna did as he requested until her heart rate returned to normal. Jess helped her to sit up, looking at her carefully. "How are you doing?" he asked gently.

Instead of responding she continued to grasp his hand tightly. She wanted to scream, fall into his arms and cry uncontrollably but something inside wouldn't let her. Instead tears silently flowed down her cheeks and she nodded to let Jess know she was okay.

Jess stroked her wet, tangled hair, surprised by how natural the gesture felt. In that moment he honestly couldn't remember why they didn't get along.

Rosanna finally pulled back, somewhat embarrassed. "What do we do now?" she asked softly.

Jess sighed. "I don't know," he admitted. "We can't go to the cops…" He trailed off, looking around. "We need to get out of here, get dried off." He stood, then held his hand out to her.

Rosanna stood shakily, leaning on him for support. Then, they slowly made their way up the rocky bank.

***

"How much cash do you have on you?"

Rosanna stared at Jess. "I don't know. Why don't we go back to the bridge and search my bag?" she asked sarcastically.

"Oh. Right." Jess reached into his back pocket, pulling out his sodden wallet. "I can't believe I didn't lose this." He quickly counted the bills, then hastily looked around the area. "There's a motel up there," he said, pointing up the hill. "We can stay there for the night, get some sleep."

"Then what?"

"Then we take advantage of the fact that they probably think we're dead, use that time to figure out what to do next. Come on."

The motel was deserted, except for the clerk behind the check-in desk, who lowered his magazine at the sound of the door.

He looked somewhat amused that they were drenched from head-to-toe, but made no comment. He accepted payment and wordlessly handed then their room key before returning to his magazine.

Jess led the way into a small, musty-smelling room, tossing the key on the bureau next to the wall. There were two twin beds a couple of feet apart, separated by a night table with a lamp and digital clock. A small TV sat on top of the bureau across from the beds, and a tiny bathroom and closet were visible at the opposite end of the room.

"You're freezing," Jess said to Rosanna, noticing she was shaking. "Maybe you should go take a hot shower. Warm up."

"What about you?"

"I'll take one after."

"Okay." Rosanna took off her soaked black leather jacket and draped it over a chair, then kicked off her shoes. "I see robes in the closet," she told him. "I don't know how sanitary they are but it'll give our clothes a chance to dry."

Jess nodded. "I would say we should hit up an ATM tomorrow but they can track us that way. Luckily I just cashed my check; we can use that for necessities."

Rosanna stopped on her way to the bathroom. "How long will we be…on the run like this?"

"I don't know." Jess sat on one of the beds. "Until we can figure out who to trust with what really happened."

"Maybe we should just keep our mouths shut," Rosanna suggested. "It might be safer that way."

"Rosanna, we saw a man murdered right in front of us. By cops no less. We can't just do nothing."

She sighed. "I know. I'm just…worried."

"So am I," he admitted.

Rosanna disappeared into the bathroom then and a few moments later, Jess could hear the sound of running water. He leaned back on the bed and grabbed the TV remote off the night table, knowing a distraction from everything was the best remedy for the moment.

The water pressure was low but the temperature was hot and Rosanna just stood for a moment under the warm spray, letting the steam relax her tense, sore muscles and calm her shaky nerves. For a brief moment she forgot the horrific murder she witnessed, nearly drowning in the river, and being terrified out of her mind.

Jess idly flipped through the channels, not finding anything of interest. Then he stopped, a breaking news report catching his eye.

A female reporter was standing in front of the spot where Jess and Rosanna had leapt from, the area now sealed off with yellow "caution" tape. Jess's blood ran cold when he saw the reporter turn to the man next to her, identifying him as Detective Tom Orson.

The man was in his late forties and had thinning, gray-streaked dark hair and eyes sharp as a flint. He was also the same man who shot a man in cold blood before pulling a gun on Rosanna.

"Can you tell us what happened here tonight, Detective?" the reporter inquired, holding
the microphone out to him.

Detective Orson nodded, looking grim. "I was out on a nearby call when my fellow officers and I spotted a young woman and a young man standing near the bridge. They both looked frightened and caught off guard when we approached. We tried to talk them down but they suddenly turned and jumped, with no explanation."

"Do you have any idea who the man and woman are?"

"We found this on the ground a few yards away." Detective Orson held up a small, black designer bag.

Jess groaned out loud when he produced Rosanna's wallet, complete with her driver's license. *Great. Now they know she is, and it won't take them long to figure out who I am. We're screwed.*

"What's the matter?"

Jess jumped slightly at Rosanna's voice. He sat up on the bed as she walked past the closet. Her long, dark hair was wet from the shower and she was wearing the thin, white terrycloth robe she'd procured from the closet earlier. Clearing his throat to get his thoughts back on track Jess nodded to the TV. "We've made breaking news," he told her. "And they've I.D.ed you."

Rosanna swore, sitting on the available bed. "That'll make it that much easier to find us. Unless they really believe we're dead."

"They're talking about a search-and-rescue," Jess informed her. "To cover their asses I'm sure."

"It's a good cover, the perfect way to track us down." Rosanna paused. "Should we call somebody?"

"Like who?"

"My sister. She must be going crazy right now, wondering why I never showed up for dinner and why I'm not answering my phone. And your brother, let them know we're both okay."

Jess was tempted but shook his head. "We can't. Not yet anyway. It's too risky."

"For us or for them?"

"For all of us."

"Alright. I just hate putting her through this." Rosanna laid back on the bed. "You're free to take a shower now." She closed her eyes. "Maybe I can go to sleep and forget any of this ever happened."

Jess shook his head. "Good luck with that."

When he got out of the shower Rosanna was asleep, burrowed under the covers. Jess turned off the TV and got into his own bed, trying to get comfortable.

At first he tried staring at the peeling paint on the ceiling but all it did was make his already troubled mind work overtime, trying to piece everything together. He rolled over, facing Rosanna's bed.

She was facing him as well, her long hair splayed haphazardly over the white pillow. Strangely enough the sight of him watching her sleep made him feel sleepy as well.

He knew they both needed all the rest they could.

Chapter Three

"I don't care about your procedure! This is Brooklyn. My sister could be lying in a ditch somewhere and you keep telling me to wait?" Nora asked in outrage.

"I'm sorry, ma'am. You'll just have to wait until a detective is available to speak to you." The receptionist pointed to the lobby. "Please have a seat."

Sighing in resignation, Nora turned and walked to the lobby, taking a seat by the window. It was one o'clock in the morning and she was sitting at the police station, waiting for someone with a badge to give her at least five minutes so she could talk about her sister.

She'd waited in the restaurant for two hours, hoping to reach Rosanna on her cell but she wasn't responding. Rosanna always kept her phone on and rarely missed calls, especially Nora's, often joking about Nora's tendency to worry. "I can't help it," Nora would say. "It's just been the two of us in the same city for so long that I turned into a mother hen." It didn't help that Nora could recall the trouble Rosanna got into when she was a teenager, making concern Nora's new middle name. Some habits were hard to let go of.

But this was far beyond being a worrywart. No one had heard from Rosanna in five hours. She wasn't at her apartment, never showed up at the restaurant, and the shop said she never brought the car part in. Nora had been all over town, finally ending up at the police station, which was virtually deserted. Apparently a couple of headcases jumped off the bridge several hours ago, and everyone was searching the river for them. Nora hadn't been paying too much attention to the details while she was waiting, nor had she listened to the radio on the car ride over; she'd been too busy on the phone.

With another impatient sigh she looked up at the TV mounted on the far wall, tuned in to the local news station. They were still talking about the bridge-jumpers and were about to identify them.

"…and again, the young woman has been identified as Rosanna Howard-"

Nora bolted from her chair and ran closer to the TV, praying she heard the newscaster incorrectly. Her heart sank into her chest when they showed an enlarged picture of Rosanna's driver's license.

"The mystery of her male counterpart has also been solved," the reporter continued. "We've received footage taken from the security camera at Mason Auto of Ms. Howard and the man Detective Orson has identified as the man who jumped with her." A freeze-frame of the image filled the screen and Nora stared at it in shock. "Jess?" she whispered in disbelief. Sure enough, the reporter confirmed the man in the video was Jess Coleman, and another picture of Nora's former brother-in-law filled the screen.

Trying to compose herself, Nora squared her shoulders and walked back over to the receptionist. "Ma'am-" she began in exasperation.

"I have information about the people who jumped off the bridge," Nora broke in shakily.

The woman raised her eyebrows in response. "What do you know about that?"

"I know the man they're saying jumped used to be my brother-in-law," Nora told her, gripping the edge of the desk so tightly her knuckles turned white. "And the woman is my little sister."

***

Rosanna was suffocating.

Everywhere she turned there was darkness, compounded by deafening silence. She tried in vain to force her lungs to cooperate but to no avail; she couldn't get any fresh air.

And it was killing her.

"Rosanna!"

Rosanna's eyes flew open and she sat up straight, gasping for air. Jess was kneeling next to the bed, trying to coax her to breathe normally. Rosanna managed to shake her head, unable to get any sound out.

Jess climbed onto the bed and sat next to her, gently pulling her back toward him. "Breathe with me," he told her, squeezing her hand. "Squeeze my hand until it passes."

Rosanna managed a nod, squeezing back.

"Don't think about anything about matching your breathing to mine," Jess said firmly. "Just focus on breathing in and out, okay?""

Rosanna did as instructed, riding out her hyperventilation. When her breathing slowed to a more natural rhythm and her heart rate returned to normal, she spoke. "I thought I was back in the water, drowning." She shuddered. "I know it sounds crazy…"

"No it doesn't. You just had a panic attack because you almost drowned. You don't just get over things like that."

Rosanna sighed. "It's not just that," she admitted. She turned to face him. "We're in so much trouble, Jess. I don't know how we're going to get out."

They were both laying on the bed now, facing one another. Rosanna was still holding Jess's hand. "That doesn't sound like the girl who punched Ronnie Williamson in the face our sophomore year at NYU."

Rosanna burst out laughing at the memory. "I haven't thought about that in years. I can't believe you remember that."

"How could I forget? It was right in the middle of the quad in broad daylight. I think you broke his nose." Jess smiled as he pictured the smart-ass jock holding his nose, blood pouring down his chin. "I can't remember why you hit him though."

Rosanna's eyes narrowed, feeling just as indignant as she had eight years ago. "I met him through Kyle and introduced him to my roommate. Six months into the relationship she found out he was cheating on her."

"That's right. I forgot he and Kyle were roommates." Jess shook his head. "You had one hell of a right hook."

"Still do. My dad always said it was important his daughters learn how to throw a good punch, in case any man was asking for it. Bet you thought I went a tad overboard, huh?"

"Actually, I thought Williamson was a jackass who totally deserved it, even though I didn't know what it was for. I bet he never cheated on any of your friends again."

"I think I cured him of that. And I didn't mean to break his nose; I felt bad about it. But no one gave me or my friends a hard time again." She paused. "Except you."

Jess shrugged. "Someone had to. Glad I never earned the wrath of a punch."

"I can't say I was never tempted. I never met anyone who liked to push my buttons as much as you."

"Back at you." He paused. "Feeling better?"

"Definitely a lot calmer. How did you know to calm me down that way?"

"I used to have panic attacks when I flew," he told her. "One day one of the other passengers was nice enough to help me through it the way I helped you."

Rosanna blinked, surprised at his honesty. Still, she was feeling more than a little awkward about what happened and let go of his hand. "Thanks. I guess we should try to get some sleep." She glanced at the clock next to her. "It's four-thirty. We shouldn't sleep too late."

Jess nodded his agreement. "Staying in one place too long isn't smart. We'll cut out of here early. And as soon as I figure out a way for it to be safe, we'll contact Nora and Eric."

"Alright. You can go back to your bed now, I'm alright," she told him.

Jess got up and went to his bed. "You're not used to anyone seeing you like that, are you?"

"Like what?"

"Vulnerable."

Rosanna stiffened. "I had a weak moment. Now I want to put it behind me. Let's get some sleep." Secretly, she *was* embarrassed that Jess of all people had seen her break down that way, but she'd never admit it.

Nor would she admit how good he'd been at calming her down.

"Now I remember," Jess said, staring at the ceiling. "Williamson started dating that girl from L.A. I don't condone cheating and I hate to admit it but Megan Foster *was* pretty hot…"

Rosanna reached under her head and grabbed one of the pillows, flinging it across the room at Jess. She was pleased to see it hit him squarely in the face.

"Good night, Rosanna," he said, his voice muffled by the pillow.

"Good night, Jess," she said back, closing her eyes.

"At least it wasn't a punch," Jess muttered into the darkness.

***

"Ms. Howard?"

Nora rose from her chair in the lobby as the receptionist beckoned her over. "Yes?"

"Two detectives are on their way to speak with you."

Nora nodded. "Thank you." She leaned against the wall, glancing at the early morning light coming in through the window. No one had been able to talk to her so Nora had gone home but didn't sleep. Promptly at six a.m. she left, coming straight back to the police station. She'd been sitting in the lobby for an hour, watching the news while she waited. So far, there was nothing new to report.

What the hell happened? Nora wondered, closing her eyes. *What on Earth possessed my sister to jump off a bridge? None of this makes any sense!*

"Holding up the wall?"

Nora's eyes snapped open at the familiar voice, the voice she spent most of her time trying to forget. "Eric," she said briskly, her voice betraying no emotion while she adjusted the strap of her purse, avoiding his eyes.

"I just heard on the radio something about my brother and your sister jumping off a bridge! What the hell's going on?" Eric demanded.

"I don't know," Nora admitted. "Two detectives are on their way to talk to me."

"I can't believe this," Eric said, shaking his head. "They have to have this wrong. Jess wouldn't jump off a bridge."

"Neither would Rosanna." Nora looked over Eric's shoulder to see a man and a woman approaching them. "Detectives? Have you found out anything about my sister?"

"Ms. Howard, I'm Detective Matthews," the woman told Nora. "This is my partner, Detective Orson." Her eyes traveled to Eric.

"I'm Eric Frost," he said, stepping forward. "I'm Jess Coleman's older brother."

Detective Orson nodded. "I see the resemblance in both of you. Why don't we all go back to my office?"

Eric and Nora followed the detectives to Detective Orson's office, sitting at a table across from the two of them. "Will you please tell us what's going on?" Nora asked. "I spent most of the night here and couldn't get a straight answer."

"I was out on a call," Detective Orson told Nora and Eric. "On my way back I saw a man and a woman standing on the edge of the bridge. They both looked scared and nervous and refused to climb down. Without any warning, they jumped."

"We've been searching the river ever since," Detective Matthews continued. She exchanged a look with her partner. "It's been nine hours," she said reluctantly. "At this point it seems likely that it will be a recovery-"

"Hold it," Eric interrupted, holding up his hand. "Let me see if I got this straight. You're saying Jess and Rosanna jumped off a bridge in the dead of winter into a river with pretty strong currents this time of year with absolutely no provocation, and no one else saw any of this. Now, because it's been nine hours, you're automatically assuming they're dead, and we-their family members-are just being brought in on this?"

"Mr. Frost-" Detective Matthews began.

"Eric's right," Nora interrupted. "We know our siblings very well and there's no way either of them would jump off a bridge of their own volition. They're not thrill-seekers, they've got great careers, friends, and busy lives…neither of them are that unstable."

"You're sure about that?" Detective Orson asked.

"One hundred percent."

"We're sorry for upsetting you," Detective Matthews told Nora and Eric. "We're just letting you know what we know."

"Have either of you considered they're afraid of something?" Eric demanded. "Maybe they were running from someone, like a mugger, got cornered and jumping off a bridge was their only way out."

"My sister's terrified of heights," Nora added. "There's no way she'd voluntarily jump off a bridge. There had to be extreme circumstances."

"And another thing," Eric went on. "There is the possibility they survived the jump and were basically unharmed, which is why you haven't found them."

"If that's the case Mr. Frost why haven't either of them contacted you?" Detective Orson asked quietly.

"I don't know," Eric admitted. "But there's more to this, I'm sure of it." He looked at Nora. "If you find out anything else please contact me and my wi-Ms. Howard," he amended hastily.

Nora understood immediately, rising. "I'll have my phone on. Call anytime." She stood, hurriedly following Eric out of the office.

Elaine Matthews leaned back in her chair, thoughtful. "Why were they in such a hurry to get out of here?" she wondered.

Tom Orson shrugged. "You got me."

"I think they might be onto something," Elaine told him. "They both seem convinced those two wouldn't jump unless prompted. Maybe they were on the run from someone."

"Maybe. Or maybe they did something to be on the run from," Tom suggested.

"Why did you want out of there so fast?" Nora demanded as Eric pulled her down the hall.

"Because none of this adds up," Eric said in a low voice, glancing carefully around. "Did you hear that Orson guy's account of what happened? It sounded just like it did on the radio."

"So?"

"So it sounds rehearsed. All of it's flimsy, Nora. Why is he so quick to write them off as dead?"

"What are you getting at?" Nora asked as they passed through the lobby.

"Something's not right," Eric told her. "I don't trust Orson. My gut's screaming at me not to. He's the only detective who saw what happened, and he's not being very helpful."

"Why wouldn't he want to find out the truth?"

"I don't know," Eric told her as they headed for the door. "Maybe it's because I'm naturally suspicious or maybe I'm not inclined to trust anyone so willing to instantly write off my brother." He opened the door for Nora and then followed her through it.

Detective Steven Frye stepped out from behind the column in the lobby, his cup of coffee forgotten in his hand, frowning at what he overheard. Like the young man, he too didn't trust Detective Orson, and had a good reason why. He just didn't have proof.

"I'm going back to the river, see if I can be any help," Elaine told Tom, putting on her jacket. "you're going to run the background checks?"

Tom nodded. "I'll let you know if I find anything." He sat down in front of his computer.

When Elaine left he did exactly that, looking up everything he could find on Rosanna Howard and Jess Coleman. Then his cell phone began to ring. He checked the number, discovering it was Nix. "Anything?" he demanded gruffly.

"Not so far. I've got Ellis, Floyd, and Allison checking out different areas. I'm closest to the river, at a bank they could've easily climbed up on."

"Keep your eyes open," Tom barked. "Most likely they're fish food but if they're not, you and the others know what to do." He paused. "You took care of it?" he asked, his voice low.

"Yes sir. There's nothing left connecting us to Sorenson."

"Except a couple of civilians with bad timing," Tom muttered, staring at Jess and Rosanna's pictures on the screen.

"Don't worry, we'll handle it. We'll come up with something," Nix said confidently.

"You better." Tom ended the call.

He turned back to the computer screen and read everything on record about Jess and Rosanna. Both their records were clean; two upstanding citizens of Brooklyn with successful careers and siblings who used to be married.

But no one was that lily-white. There had to be something he could use.

It had to be his top priority.

***

"Alright," Jess told Rosanna, stopping outside the small consignment shop. "We go in, find clothes we'd normally never wear and hats. As quickly as possible."

Rosanna nodded. "You're really good at this cloak-and-dagger stuff. Have you been on the run from the cops before?"

"No," Jess said defensively. "I watched a lot of NYPD Blue in college."

Rosanna shook her head and followed him into the store.

Staying close together they each selected nondescript jeans, T-shirts, hoodies, and plain ball caps before going into the dressing rooms to change. After changing, Rosanna stared at her reflection, carefully pulling her long ponytail through her ball cap. She barely recognized herself out of her dressy, upscale attire she wore to work daily. She wondered about her co-workers, her friends, who'd more than likely heard the news by now, wondered how they'd react and what they'd be thinking. She sat down and laced up her plain white sneakers thinking about everyone she knew and cared about: her friends, Nora, her parents…what would they all think about what was going on? She knew Nora would be a wreck, her parents as well.

She wondered briefly if her ex-fiance knew about the situation, or if he even cared.

Taking one last look at herself in the unfamiliar yet comfortable ensemble and her tired expression, complete with dark circles under her eyes, she called out to Jess in the room next to her. "You ready?"

Before Jess answered he looked at his worn expression, suddenly feeling much older than his twenty-eight years. Worry lines creased his forehead, refusing to completely disappear. He slid the ball cap over his matted dark blonde hair. "Yeah," he called back finally. "Let's get out of here."

When they left the store they began to walk down the sidewalk, remaining watchful. "What should we do now?" Rosanna wanted to know. "Lay low?"

Jess nodded. "As much as we can. We have to figure out who we can go to about this. Not friends, not family. It's too dangerous to get them involved."

"Maybe we should do a little research on what we know," she suggested. "Find more out about what we've gotten ourselves into."

"Good idea. There's a library not too far from here, so we can have access to a computer."

When they arrived at the library Rosanna sat at the computer with Jess at her side, typing in the name DARRELL EMERY. "I know this name," she told Jess. "His murder was all over the news for the past couple of weeks." She paused. "By the way…thank you."

"For what?"

"For saving my life in the river," she told him. "So much has happened that I haven't gotten a chance to say anything-"

"You don't have to," Jess interrupted. "It's what anyone would've done."

There was an awkward silence as Rosanna scrolled through the search results. Then she cleared her throat. "Here's something interesting. He was a computer analyst brought in by the cops to help with a case."

"What case?"

"The murder of that judge's wife a while back, Carolyn Warren. The case was handled by Elaine Matthews and her partner…Tom Orson."

"The first connection."

"It says here Darrell was on the verge of finding evidence in the case when he was killed. Carolyn Warren was suspected of having ties to drug dealers; she was reportedly seen with the well-known but never caught drug lord, Dex Angelo, a few weeks before her death. He fled the state not long after that. It also says he had a contact named Paul Sorenson." She froze after she clicked on the photo. "Does he look familiar to you?"

"Holy crap," Jess breathed. "That's the guy Orson killed in front of us." He looked at Rosanna. "What do you think?"

"I think Orson was involved somehow in Carolyn Warren's murder," she replied. "Darrell Emery found the evidence so Orson had him killed to shut him up.Sorenson too. Anyone involved in this is either dead or missing."

"No loose ends." Jess sighed. "Except us."

"Okay. So we know Emery knew something, we just don't know what. We need proof linking Orson to his murder, Sorenson's, and Carolyn's." She looked over at Jess. "Up for a little detective work?"

"What do you have in mind?"

"The article says Darrell is survived by his fiancée, Lisa Woodward, here in Brooklyn. Maybe we should go talk to her."

Jess nodded. "Maybe we should. But first we need a game plan."

As Jess and Rosanna exited the library a man looked up a few yards away, casually leaning up against his car. Reaching into his pocket, he pulled out his phone. "It's Nix," he said. "I found them."

Chapter Four

Tom hung up with Nix just as Elaine entered his office. "A witness just spotted two people matching Coleman and Howard's descriptions leaving the public library on 32nd-"

"What witness?"

"He left just now. Early thirties, riding a scooter nearby. He saw the missing persons bit on the news-"

"I still think that's a waste of time, calling them 'missing persons'," Tom interrupted. "You know what the chances are of them being alive. This person was probably just a crank like the others."

"Maybe. But we should still check it out."

"Nix is already in the area," Tom said quickly. "I'll radio him and let him know where to look."

"Alright. Let me know what you find out." Elaine left the office.

Tom immediately picked up his phone. "Allison? It's Orson. You and Floyd get down here. I have an inquisitive partner who needs to be distracted. Yeah, Nix is already on it. He'll call Ellis if he needs backup."

Elaine was walking down the hall to her office when she was stopped by Steven Frye, a detective who transferred from Manhattan a few months ago. Rumor had it that he was a good cop, quick on his feet, but had a hard time keeping a partner due to his inability to collaborate, as she knew all too well.

"You got a minute?" Frye asked, falling into step beside her. "I need to run something

"Frye, I'm up to my ears in the Howard and Coleman investigation-"

"That's what this is about, in a way," he told her. "It won't take long, I promise."

"Alright," Elaine responded, surprised. "In my office."

She closed the door behind him and gestured for him to sit down in front of her desk. "What's going on?"

"How well do you know your partner, Matthews?"

Elaine blinked, put off by his bluntness. "Pretty well. We've been working together for about a year, when I was transferred from Jersey. Why do you ask?" Her tone was somewhat suspicious.

Frye quickly repeated the conversation he overheard between Eric Frost and Nora Howard. Elaine listened thoughtfully. "I've always stood by my partners one hundred percent," she told Frye after a moment. "You have to in our line of work. Tom's never given me reason to doubt him or his ability to do the job. I get a lot of crap sometimes when I work with men but Tom's always treated me like an equal, always had my back. That being said…something's off about this case. Tom is being a little too quick to pronounce them both dead for my comfort but I'm sure he has his reasons. It doesn't mean I don't trust him." She looked carefully at Frye. "It's obvious you don't' share my belief."

"I don't know anyone here that well, but I did work with you and Orson on the Carolyn Warren murder investigation."

"I remember you weren't too happy about working with us."

"Nothing personal," he assured her. "I haven't had a partner in a while and am used to working alone. I have to tell you…that case never sat well with me."

"I put a hundred percent into that investigation," Elaine said defensively. "I can assure you we did everything we could to find out who was responsible. It was a high-profile case; a lot of pressure was on us. Even though we still haven't wrapped up everything we know Carolyn was having involved with Dex Angelo, possibly in the drug ring he started. There's an outstanding warrant for his arrest but it's obvious he left the country and we can't touch him on foreign soil. We're also still looking for Paul Sorenson, who was in this up to his eyeballs. Darrell Emery must have been able to tie it all in together, which is why someone shut him up, possibly Sorenson. Or Angelo. Who knows how many people were involved in this."

"You never found it odd how quickly the evidence started to point to Angelo and Sorenson?"

"It wasn't that much of a stretch. Every cop in the city knows Angelo's one of the top drug dealers in the area but nothing's ever been able to stick." Elaine frowned. "What's this got to do with Howard and Coleman? The only thing both cases have in common is they're mine and Tom's cases."

"Exactly."

"I don't like what you're implying, Detective Frye. Why are you suddenly on a witch hunt for my partner?"

"It's not sudden," Frye said abruptly. "I've had suspicions about Tom Orson since I started working here."

"Why?"

"I'm not sure I trust you enough yet to let you know." He stood. "I've got good instincts, Matthews. That's why I'm still alive. And right now they're telling me something's not right with your partner."

"How do you know I won't go straight down the hall and tell him what you're telling me?" Elaine wanted to know.

"I don't," Frye told her honestly. "If that's what you want to do, I won't stop you. But I can tell you have questions too. Maybe should mull them over before you run and talk to your partner." Frye left.

Elaine sat where she was, unsure of what to think. Tom had been a good partner, and a good friend. Just because he'd been acting strangely lately didn't mean she should treat Frye's suspicions with any validity.

A knock sounded on the door then. "Come in," she called wearily.

Officer Dennis Floyd and Officer Kenneth Allison walked in, approaching her quickly. "Detective Orson told us we should start contacting more of Howard and Coleman's friends and family, see what more we can find out about them."

"I was about to get started on that," she told them, pushing the conversation with Frye from her mind. "Why don't we start with the co-workers."

***

"When do you want to see Lisa Woodward?" Rosanna asked Jess as they walked away from 32nd street.

"I think we should get something to eat first," Jess told her. "We're both running on fumes."

"Alright," Rosanna agreed. "I vote fast-food, get in and get out real quick."

Jess agreed. "What's your preference?"

"I don't care, I'm starving." Rosanna nodded up the hill. "I see a McDonald's."

"You know, I never figured you for a fast-food type," Jess commented as they walked. "You seem more like the broccoli and eggplant type."

Rosanna raised an eyebrow. "Me?" she asked in disbelief. "I've never eaten broccoli or eggplant in my life. I'm a total cheeseburger and fries kind of girl."

"You learn something new every day," Jess quipped. "Can we pick up the pace a little? I haven't eaten in twelve hours."

"Neither have I," Rosanna retorted. "Which is why I'm not moving at the speed of light."

"And explains your sunny disposition."

"Shut up!" Rosanna snapped, feeling her self-control vanish. "You're the whole reason we're in this mess."

Jess stopped in his tracks. "Excuse me?"

"You heard me. If you hadn't been pestering me at the auto store, begging me to make my sister give your two-timing brother another chance I wouldn't have been distracted. I wouldn't have been anywhere near that alley; I would've been on my way to the restaurant to meet my sister instead of stumbling on a murder, by cops no less."

"You're a real piece of work, you know that?" Jess followed her as she began to stalk off. "If you didn't have a temper from hell neither one of us would've been in that alley."

Rosanna stopped, whirling on him. "I had every right to be pissed at you because you had *no* right coming to me on your brother's behalf. If he's really sorry, he should tell Nora himself. Not get his brother to do his dirty work for him."

Jess shook his head. "You're incredible. You always find a way to bring everything back on my brother. He's human, Rose. He made a mistake. Are you really so arrogant that you can't understand that?"

"Of course I understand mistakes," Rosanna shot back, insulted. "But this is about my sister, the sweetest, most thoughtful and generous person on the planet. She trusted Eric, loved him more than any man in the world. Can you honestly say he felt the same way about her?"

"Of course he did," Jess said, following her down a sidewalk to a dead-end. "Love's not perfect you know. You can still screw things up. It didn't mean he stopped loving her."

Rosanna snorted. "He had a funny way of showing it."

Jess threw his hands up in the air. "I give up. You're the most stubborn, infuriating person I've ever met. Even in college, you always had to have everything the 'Rosanna way'. If people didn't act exactly the way you wanted them to, to hell with them. That's why we never got along, that's why your engagement to Kyle Lucas lasted three seconds."

Rosanna stopped, backing slightly away. "Who do you think you are?" she demanded quietly. "You don't know jack about my relationship with Kyle or why it ended. And do you really think you're so perfect in relationships? You never had one last longer than a couple of months because you were too scared to ever let anyone really see you. You hide behind perversion and quips, never letting anyone get too close. That's why we never got along. You kept me-and everyone else-at arm's length."

Jess shook his head. "You don't know what you're talking about. And you sure as hell don't know me."

"And you don't know me," Rosanna said quietly.

"It's really a shame to hear couples argue."

Jess and Rosanna stopped dead in their tracks as a uniformed cop slowly walked toward them, his gun drawn. They instinctively clasped hands, slowly backing into the dead end, surrounded by deserted, dilapidated buildings. They immediately recognized him as one of the cops working with Orson.

"Down here, Ellis," he called and another cop appeared behind him, his gun also drawn. "You finally found them Nix," he called back. "I was starting to get worried."

Nix focused his attention on Jess and Rosanna. "In the wrong place at the wrong time," he told them. "It's too bad really."

"Too bad for us you mean," Rosanna muttered.

Nix chuckled. "Smartass. I like that." His expression hardened. "Here's how it's going to go down. You two were on the run after attempting to knock over a liquor store-Ellis and I will swear to it-when we caught you at the bridge last night. In your panic you jumped into the river and amazingly survived. Unfortunately you resisted arrest when we found you, assaulted us, and were shot trying to escape." He aimed his gun.

"No one will ever believe that," Jess told him. "Our records are clean; we've never been in trouble with the law before."

"Let us worry about that," Nix said. "It won't matter much to either of you."

Jess eyed Rosanna, then abruptly dropped her hand. "Don't kill me because of something she did," he said quickly, giving her an irritated glance.

Rosanna's eyes widened in surprise until she realized what he was doing. "Something I did?" she repeated loudly. "I think we already established it was your fault we were in that alley."

"My fault?" Jess echoed incredulously, stepping back from her. "You have no sense of direction and you're blaming me?"

"Shoot them!" Ellis yelled. "They're so loud someone will hear."

Nix jerked his head backward to face him. "Will you stop worrying-"

In that moment Jess lunged forward, overpowering Nix while they wrestled for the gun. Rosanna fought off Ellis, who grabbed her roughly by the hair, causing her to cry out.

The cry only distracted Jess momentarily and he managed to get the gun from Nix. He punched him in the face and grabbed Rosanna from Ellis, who knocked the gun from his hand.

"Run!" Jess yelled at Rosanna as Ellis began to shoot.

As they took off they heard Nix's voice in the background as he spoke into his radio, claiming they assaulted him and Ellis before escaping.

"Why aren't they following us?" Rosanna asked after a moment as they continued to run.

"I don't know. Keep going."

After a while they slowed down, collapsing to the ground to catch their breath. When Rosanna could finally talk she turned to Jess. "That was close," she managed. "Good idea, starting an argument to distract them." She stopped suddenly, staring at the dark red stain seeping through the shoulder of Jess's sweatshirt. "Oh my God," she cried, going to him. "You were shot."

Chapter Five

"I feel so useless, just sitting in some coffee shop," Nora said, pushing her salad listlessly around her plate. "Like I can really eat at a time like this."

"You need to try," Eric told her. "I bet you haven't eaten in close to twenty-four hours."

"What's the point? It's not helping me find my sister." Nora put her fork down and groaned in frustration. "There has to be something we can do."

"There is. Take care of ourselves so we're in good condition to take care of them when we find them," Eric told her, nudging her glass of water closer to her.

"You really believe they're still alive?" Nora asked quietly.

"The cops might not but I sure as hell do," Eric declared. "We can't give up on them. They need us to be strong."

Nora sighed. "I still don't understand what happened. Why were they together in the first place? They're not exactly best friends."

"That's an understatement."

Nora smiled suddenly. "Remember how they acted when they first found out we were engaged?"

Eric shook his head ruefully. "I think Jess's exact words were 'I'll do anything not to be related to Rosanna Howard, including having bamboo chutes shoved under my fingernails'."

Nora managed a small laugh. "Rosanna offered to take me to Europe to find a nice man with no jackass brothers. Her words." Nora sipped her water. "They did manage to put their differences aside long enough to throw us a great engagement party, and give great speeches at the wedding reception."

"That they did." Eric paused. "So you're going by Howard again, huh?"

"It's my name."

"I know. I just thought…I mean we've been divorced-officially-for a month. I guess I just thought it would take longer for you to change your name back. If you did at all."

"It's time to move on Eric," Nora said quietly. "The divorce may have only been finalized for a month but I filed last year."

"I know. The day after our fifth anniversary."

"What was I supposed to do?" she demanded, her voice rising. "I'd just caught you in a huge lie, found out you were at the center of the town's biggest scandal?"

"I know it was wrong Nora-"

"Wrong?" Nora repeated. "You had an affair with an eighteen-year-old girl, a girl still in high school. A girl thirteen years younger than you. Here we were on a nice, romantic dinner to celebrate our wedding anniversary when a couple comes up to us, calling you a predator. That's how I found out."

"I already told you how sorry I am, for all of it. Getting involved with Brittany Marsh was the biggest mistake of my entire life. Cheating on you was wrong, being with her was wrong-legal or not, she's still just a kid. I was going through a hard time-it's no excuse-but you were always working-"

"You're still blaming all of this on me?" Nora cried. "A year later and you haven't changed. You still can't accept responsibility-" Her phone rang, cutting her off. "Hello?" she asked eagerly.

"Ms. Howard? It's Detective Matthews. Is Mr. Frost still with you?"

"Yes."

"We'd like you to both come down to the station at your convenience."

A short while later they were walking down the hall to Detective Matthews's office. "We got a call earlier that Ms. Howard and Mr. Coleman were spotted at the public library on 32nd," she told them once they'd all been seated. "My partner just informed me that the library was checked but there was no trace of either of them."

"Does that mean it wasn't them?" Nora asked.

"Possibly. Or it could have been them but they were long gone by the time we arrived."

"So what now?" Eric wanted to know. "Are you still searching the river?"

"Yes, but we're also considering the possibility that they made it to shore. The library isn't far from the river-" She broke off mid-sentence when a uniformed officer burst into her office. "What is it, Officer Allison?"

"A call just came in from Nix," he told her hastily. "He said Howard and Coleman's descriptions matched those of a couple who robbed a liquor store last night. He and Ellis were in the process of arresting them when they assaulted them and fled. Coleman was wounded in the attempt, so they couldn't have gotten far."

"Get Orson in here," Detective Matthews barked. "Now."

Eric and Nora looked at each other in horror and disbelief.

* * *

While the prescient was abuzz with the latest news that Howard and Coleman were now fugitives, Detective Steven Frye took it upon himself to go into the evidence room and check the files on the Carolyn Warren murder investigation.

Frye knew something was off about the investigation, and had been since the very beginning. He didn't doubt Detective Matthews's ability; from what he'd seen she was a very diligent cop. It was Orson he didn't trust, questioning the way Orson found the evidence practically tied up neatly with a bow.

As Frye looked through the files he remembered the suspicions that Carolyn Warren was having an affair, possibly with Dex Angelo, who she was allegedly conspiring with in the drug ring scandal. But the facts didn't completely add up. Something crucial was missing.

Maybe it had something to do with the fact that Frye knew of at least one affair Carolyn Warren had been having, based on a conversation he overheard on his first day…

"Carolyn Warren? I can't investigate this," Orson was telling Floyd.

"Because-"

"Because they'll find out Dex Angelo wasn't the only one sleeping with her."

Floyd had noticed Frye then and the conversation had ceased. But Frye could tell there was a lot more they wanted to say. He'd long thought about the conversation, especially during the Carolyn Warren murder investigation. But he had no proof of anything; Orson admitting the affair was only hearsay.

But what if it hadn't stopped with the affair?

As Frye left the evidence room he was approached by Detective Tanner from down the hall. "Have you heard? They found Paul Sorenson."

"Where?"

"At the bottom of the river."

Frye quickened his pace, heading down the hall.

Chapter Six

"I don't think anyone's been here in a while," Rosanna said, peering into the dirt-streaked windows of the tiny drugstore. "This is the only window not boarded up. But there's plenty of stuff inside." She pulled her sleeve down over her hand and punched the weak glass, shattering the window.

Jess raised an eyebrow. "Look at you, breaking into a drugstore."

"The cops are claiming we robbed a liquor store and assaulted them. I don't think it'll hurt to add breaking and entering to the list." She climbed through the small window and walked to the door, unlocking it. Then she guided Jess inside.

"It's my shoulder, not my legs," he complained.

"You're bleeding, hungry, and exhausted," she reminded him, leading him down the aisle. "Now, sit down before you fall over."

"Yes ma'am."

Rosanna searched the store until she found gauze, antiseptic, and bandages. Then she went back to Jess. "Take off your sweatshirt," she ordered.

"I like 'em bossy," Jess quipped.

Rosanna rolled her eyes and helped him lift the shirt up over his head. Then she knelt down in front of him, rolling up the soaked sleeve of his T-shirt.

"How bad is it?" Jess wanted to know.

Rosanna dabbed a cotton ball in the antiseptic. "It looks like you were lucky," she said, beginning to wipe off the blood.

Jess gritted his teeth at the sting. "How's that?"

"You were nicked."

"That's all?" he demanded. "How come there's so much blood then?"

"Trust me, there'd be a lot more if the bullet went in." She wrapped the gauze around the still bleeding scratch.

"How do you know so much about this?"

"You watched cop shows in college, I watched doctor shows." She put the bandage on top. "There. Good as new." She looked around. "Do you see what I see?"

"A rat peeking at us around the corner?"

Rosanna's eyes narrowed. "That better be a joke. I was talking about all the food." She stood up. "Ready to pig out? I'll get some of everything."

"Wait." Jess grabbed her by the arm as she turned to go. "I'm sorry. And thanks."

"I'm sorry too," she told him quietly. "And your shoulder was nothing. If you'd actually been shot we'd be in even bigger trouble."

She returned a moment later with an armful of chips, cookies, drinks, and candy. She disappeared and came back with an old radio. "I saw this behind the counter. If it works we can have some tunes while we eat."

She spread out the food and drinks and set up the radio- which worked amazingly enough. "We have a feast here," she told Jess. "We've got cheese crackers, barbeque chips, chocolate cookies, vanilla wafers, bottled water, and root beer."

Jess stared at her. "Is this the whole store?" he asked, gesturing toward the food.

"I thought you might like variety," she replied. "Bon appetit."

They munched on a little of everything, talking and listening to the radio. Then Rosanna stopped. "I haven't heard this song in years."

"Neither have I. the last time I heard it was at that club near campus, Screaming Viper."

"Yeah they played it there all the time," Rosanna remembered. "The last time I was at that club was right before graduation. That was the night Kyle proposed to me."

"I remember," Jess told her. "I was there with some friends and I saw the two of you. It was easy to tell what was going on."

"That's right; you passed us as we were leaving. Kyle talked to you and you congratulated him. I remember thinking it was weird since you couldn't stand me. But since you and Kyle were friends…" She trailed off, munching on a chip.

"I really meant it," Jess told her. "Even though we didn't get along...I still thought you and Kyle were a good couple."

Rosanna stared at him in amazement. "I didn't know that."

Jess shrugged. "It was because I kept you at arm's length."

"Jess-"

"You were right," he insisted. "I've always been that way. I never let people get that close." He looked at her. "Maybe I'm a little stubborn too."

"Since we're admitting things...you weren't so off-base in what you said either," Rosanna said quietly. "I do want things to be a certain way. And I do have a temper from hell." She looked down at her hands in shame.

Jess gently lifted her chin with his finger. "Your temper makes you tough," he told her. "Tough enough to handle what we've been through in the past twenty-four hours, tough enough to handle whatever comes next."

"Maybe the reason we've never gotten along is because we're so much alike," she observed, her pulse quickening at his touch.

"Sounds about right to me." His eyes locked with hers.

Rosanna pulled away at the intensity. "It's getting dark out," she said quickly, looking out the window.

"We should get going, find somewhere to crash for the night."

"Why not crash here?" she asked. "We've got everything we need except a bed, but our jackets should provide us with enough warmth. That way we could save on money."

"It's pretty deserted around here," Jess mused. "I guess it could work. And I honestly don't feel like walking anywhere else right now."

"Me either." Rosanna jumped up. "I'll be right back."

She came back with an aluminum baseball bat. "I saw this behind the counter. They must've been afraid of people stealing or something." She smiled at the irony, placing the bat next to Jess. "For protection."

Jess shook his head. Then he cleared his throat. "First thing in the morning we should track down Lisa Woodward, start our own investigating."

Rosanna nodded. "Sounds like a plan. First, we get some much-needed sleep."

They both stretched out on the clearest part of the floor they could find, looking up at the ceiling. "I can't believe tomorrow's Friday," Rosanna said into the darkness. "This has been the longest week of my life."

"Tell me about it. It's been the longest I've gone without a cell phone."

"Me too. Without any possessions at all." She turned to Jess. "I have a confession to make."

"You secretly listen to Britney Spears?"

Rosanna punched him playfully on the arm. "No. if we weren't running from crooked cops or getting shot at...this might almost be fun. An adventure."

"I could do without all the running, but I get what you mean. No work, no phones, no cabs...kind of like another life."

"Exactly."

They lapsed into contented silence for a moment, then Jess finally broke it. "What did happen with you and Kyle?" he wanted to know. "If you don't mind me asking."

"Kyle and I were great together when we were in college," Rosanna reflected. "We wanted the same things, had the same kind of lives. But once we graduated and started really talking about marriage...things changed. We weren't going in the same direction anymore. What we had wasn't enough to last in the real world."

"How does it last?" Jess wondered.

"Beats me. Kyle was my longest relationship." She paused. "My best guess is it'll last when two people decide life won't get in the way."

The silence returned and Rosanna welcomed it. It was unsettling to talk so candidly with Jess.

Unsettling because it felt so natural.

Moments passed and Jess heard Rosanna's steady breathing, knowing she was asleep. He rolled over to face her, just watching her for a moment. Despite anything else he'd always thought of her, he had to admit she was a total knockout.

He also had to admit he might've been wrong about all the other stuff.

He scooted closer to her until they were almost touching, then closed his eyes.

Chapter Seven

"Don't you think it's time you called it a night?" Tanner asked, stopping by Frye's open door. "It's past midnight."

Frye shook his head. "Still working on the Sorenson case."

Tanner leaned against the doorframe. "What's left to work on? The bullet they pulled out of Sorenson's chest matched the gun they found earlier today, and it belonged to Dex Angelo."

"Angelo's supposedly out of the country."

"That's what he wanted us to think; hiding in plain sight is a smart move. Until he decided he couldn't run the risk of having Sorenson talk, so he plugged him."

Frye shook his head. "It's too convenient."

"Frye, sometimes an egg is just an egg. Let it go; this one's open-and-shut." He turned to go.

"Wait," Frye called after him. "Is Matthews still around?"

"She's with Orson, talking to the brother and sister of the jumpers-turned-fugitives."

Nora and Eric were sitting in Detective Matthews's office across from her and Orson, finally able to speak to them after all the running around the prescient they did for the past several hours. Unfortunately, the conversation wasn't turning out well.

"There is absolutely no way in hell my brother or Rosanna would try to hold up a liquor store," Eric told them impatiently. "And they wouldn't assault cops either. Something else has to be going on."

Elaine handed him a photograph. "This was taken from the security camera at the liquor store Wednesday evening, a half hour before they ended up at the bridge."

"That's impossible," Nora said. "You already know they were at the auto parts store."

"The time stamp reads it was before the auto store," Matthews told her.

Nora looked at the fuzzy photo Eric was holding of a young man and a young woman in hooded sweatshirts, the man pulling a gun on the cashier. All she could make out was long dark hair on the woman and dark blonde hair on the man. "This could be anyone," she declared. "You can't clearly see their faces."

"Besides, why rob a liquor store and then buy a part from an auto parts store?" Eric asked. "That doesn't add up."

"Not much of this case does," Detective Matthews agreed. "We're hoping the two of you could fill in the blanks."

"Actually," Detective Orson spoke up, "we might have more answers than you think. I pulled up each of their records, and they come up clean."

"That's what we've been telling you," Eric pointed out.

Orson nodded thoughtfully. "Yes you have. But those are just their adult records."

Nora stiffened.

"What are you getting at?" Eric wanted to know.

"Juvenile records," Orson said simply.

"Those records are sealed," Nora said through clenched teeth. Eric turned to her. "What's he talking about?"

"I'm talking about Ms. Howard's sister." Orson opened the file he'd been holding and began to read. " 'Rosanna Howard, seventeen, is charged with breaking and entering and petty theft.'"

Matthews turned to him in surprise. "You didn't tell me about this."

Eric looked similarly at Nora. "What's going on?"

Orson closed the file. "When Rosanna Howard was a teenager she broke into a closed cosmetics store and helped herself to various items."

"That's not what happened," Nora snapped. "She was with a group of friends who decided to break into the store. Rosanna waited in the car but she got nervous because they were taking so long, so she went inside. They were all caught." Nora was beginning to get angry. "That was a long time ago, and she accepted her punishment gracefully. She was a kid who made a bad judgment call. As you can see from her record now, she's way past that."

"Being present when some teenagers break into a cosmetics store is a far cry from holding up a liquor store now," Eric chimed in, and Nora looked at him gratefully.

"It shows that Ms. Howard is prone to breaking the law," Orson said. "Why is it such a stretch for her to do it again?"

"It sounds to me like you're trying to railroad my sister, and I don't appreciate it one bit." Nora stood. "I'm not going to stay here and listen to you accuse her without any hard proof any longer. If you aren't going to try to find her, I'll do it myself." She stalked out of the office, Eric following suit.

Elaine looked at Tom. "What was that?" she demanded.

"What?"

"First of all, you have to have permission from a judge to look into sealed records, which I'm sure you haven't had time to do. Second, she was right. Why are you so quick to assume Rosanna Howard is guilty?"

"She is guilty. Ellis and Nix swear to it, and she and Coleman assaulted them in order to escape. Innocent people don't do that." His phone began to ring. "It's Nix. I have to take this." Orson left the office.

"I can't believe this," Nora said as she burst through the double-doors, walking quickly down the front steps. "What kind of prescient is this? Why is it guilty until proven innocent?"

"I don't know, but all of this is screwed to hell." Eric gently grabbed her by the arm to get her to stop. "How come you never told me about Rosanna?"

"It was private, and it wasn't my place to tell. She's come a long way from her wild-child days and she's proud of it. That was in the past."

"I never would have judged her for it," Eric said quietly. "We all make mistakes."

Nora nodded. "I know you wouldn't have."

"Did you mean what you said back there? About finding her yourself?"

"Yes, I did."

"Then I'm going to find them with you."

Back inside, Elaine stopped by Frye's office. "Got a minute?"

He looked up from his paperwork. "What is it?"

Elaine walked into his office and closed the door. "I don't want to admit it…but you might be right about Tom. He's trying to railroad Howard and Coleman."

Now his interest was definitely piqued. He almost considered telling her about what he overheard between Orson and Nix but he wasn't sure he could trust her yet. Instead, he cleared his throat. "The question is, why?" He gestured to the files on his desk. "I think it's all connected: Carolyn Warren, Darrell Emery, finding Sorenson's body and having the evidence point to Angelo, and Howard and Coleman. The only thing they have in common-"

"-is Tom," Elaine finished with a sigh. "What do you want to do?"

"I'm going to see Emery's fiancée tomorrow, see if she knows anything about what he was working on before he was killed."

Elaine nodded. "I'll watch Tom, see if he slips up in any way."

"Keep an eye on Nix too. I don't think he's alone in this."

Chapter Eight

Rosanna blinked at the bright sunlight, momentarily forgetting where she was. As her eyes adjusted, she saw she wasn't in bed alone.

Jess was facing her, fast asleep.

It was then she remembered she wasn't in bed or at home; she was lying on the floor of an abandoned drugstore, on the run from murdering cops. With Jess.

Rosanna's eyes flicked downward and she saw that her hand and Jess's hand were linked. She looked back up at his face, as tired and worn as her own must be. It was incredible to think about what all they'd been through in less than forty-eight hours.

She saw Jess stir then, stretching and blinking before focusing on her. "Morning," he said sleepily.

"Morning," she said back. "Sleep okay?"

"Not bad, considering we're on the floor."

"How's your shoulder?"

"Fine," he assured her. He looked down at their clasped hands and immediately let go, sitting up. "I guess we should get going."

Rosanna sat up as well, feeling somewhat embarrassed. "Want some breakfast first? Or have you had your fill of chips and cookies for one day?"

"I'm good," he told her. "I think we need to get going if we're going to see Lisa Woodward. The address isn't close to here."

"We're going to have to be a lot more careful now," Rosanna said as they stood. "Naming us as fugitives is a way of tightening the noose; the search will be more extensive now."

Jess nodded his agreement. "You're right." He looked around the store then back at her, as if he wanted to say something more. Then he cleared his throat. "Ready?"

"Yeah." She followed Jess to the door, then took one last look around the store. Last night had been a first; she and Jess had never been so open and honest with one another before. And waking up so close to him, holding hands…it was a kind of intimacy she'd never experienced before.

Taking a breath, she followed Jess out the door without looking back.

Chapter Nine

Frye walked up the steps to a small house that Friday around noon. He knocked briskly on Lisa Woodward's door, waiting.

A woman in her late twenties answered, her expression unreadable. "May I help you?"

"Lisa Woodward?"

"Yes?"

"I'm Detective Frye." He held out his badge. "I'd like to talk to you about your late fiancé."

Lisa stepped aside, letting him walk inside. "What would you like to know?" She gestured for him to sit across from her on the couch.

"Did Mr. Emery happen to confide in you about what he was working on before he died?"

"Some of it, yes. He needed a sounding board."

"What did he tell you?"

"That Carolyn Warren was involved in the drug ring. In fact, she and Dex Angelo were running it."

"Anything else?"

"Like what?"

"Did Mr. Emery say if Carolyn Warren was having an affair?"

"Yes, with Dex Angelo."

"Was that the only affair?"

"As far as I know."

Frye nodded thoughtfully. "I see."

"Have you gotten any closer to finding out who killed my fiancé, Detective?" Lisa wanted to know.

"We're working on it, Ms. Woodward. Thank you for your time." Frye stood. "One more thing."

Lisa waited for him to continue.

"Did Mr. Emery back up anything he was working on?"

"I don't know," Lisa replied. "If he did, he didn't tell me."

"If you think of anything else, let me know." Frye handed her his card. "Have a good day, Ms. Woodward."

After Lisa shut the door she stood at the window, watching until Frye drove away. "It's okay," she called, turning around. "You can come out now."

Jess and Rosanna emerged from the back room, walking down the hallway. "Thanks for hiding us," Jess told Lisa, and Rosanna nodded.

"It's the least I can do, since you're looking into Darrell's death. He told me not to trust the cops."

Jess and Rosanna exchanged a glance. They both agreed to keep the identity of Darrell's murderer a secret from Lisa, to protect her.

"Anyway, like I was telling you before the detective showed up, Darrell kept a safety deposit box, since he didn't trust the cops. I didn't tell them about it. I've been working up the courage to open it…maybe today's the day."

"We'd go with you," Rosanna began, "but we have to lay low right now."

"I understand. You're welcome to wait here until I get back. Clean up, help yourselves to the kitchen, whatever you need," Lisa offered.

"Thanks," Rosanna told her sincerely. "We really appreciate it."

After Lisa left Rosanna turned to Jess. "What do you think about Detective Frye?"

"I don't know. Why was he so interested in Carolyn Warren? That wasn't his case. Then he's looking into Darrell's murder…" He trailed off. "Either he's in on it with Orson and he's covering his bases or he suspects Orson. Question is, which is it?"

"I don't know. He wasn't there that night, when Orson killed Sorenson." Rosanna groaned. "All of this is giving me a headache."

"Why don't you take a shower?" Jess suggested. "Maybe it'll help."

"I guess. Lisa said we could…but it still feels strange." She walked back to the bathroom.

Jess sank onto the couch, closing his eyes. Trying to piece everything together was getting to him too, making him more exhausted than he already was.

He could hear the faint sound of the shower in the back, and his thoughts strayed to Rosanna. After everything that had happened, only one thing was becoming clear to him.

He didn't hate Rosanna.

Yes, she could push his buttons like no one else could and could be unbelievably irritating at times but when it came down to it, he didn't want anything to happen to her. And last night…it wasn't terrible waking up next to her. In fact, he kind of liked it.

A lot.

The next thing he knew, Rosanna was gently shaking his shoulder. "Jess," she said softly. "Wake up."

Jess blinked, looking at her half-dried hair. "How long was I asleep?"

"Almost an hour. Lisa's still not back."

"The bank isn't close by," he reminded her, sitting up. "I think I'll go take a shower now."

"I'll get us some food."

In the bathroom Jess took off his bandage, examining his shoulder in the mirror. It didn't look bad at all, probably because Rosanna did such a good job of patching him up.

He felt some of the tension melt away in the hot steam, and he tried to forget all the concerns pressing him. When he emerged he found Rosanna setting out sandwiches in the kitchen.

When they were nearly finished eating Lisa returned home, handing them a flashdrive. "This is it."

"Maybe we should look at it, since we're already in this up to our ears," Jess told her. "Keep you out of it, keep you safe."

"We should get going," Rosanna added. "We've already put you at risk, being here as long as we have."

"Wait." Lisa left the room and retuned with a laptop computer. "This was one of Darrell's," she said softly. "Take it, hook up the flashdrive, and find out what you need to know."

"We promise to get this into the right hands," Jess told her. "As soon as we figure out who we can trust."

"Thanks for everything," Rosanna added. "You've been so kind to us."

"You're welcome. And good luck."

They checked into an out-of-the-way roadside motel so they would have somewhere to sleep that night, and privacy to find out what was on the flashdrive. They sat down on the bed and Jess plugged it into the USB port, and they waited.

Jess whistled. "Damn," he muttered. Rosanna peered over his shoulder, reading.

Darrell had information about everything, the whole situation. Orson was Carolyn's true partner in the drug ring; Angelo was more of a silent partner. Orson and Carolyn were also having an affair. Orson brought four officers in on it: Nix, Ellis, Floyd, and Allison, with lucrative promises of profits. Carolyn eventually wanted out but wasn't sure if she could trust Angelo, so she confided in Orson instead, who turned on her and killed her.

"He took the case to clean up loose ends," Rosanna guessed. "And it worked at first-he blamed the whole thing on Angelo. But then Emery was brought in and found out the truth."

Jess nodded. "So Orson went to Sorenson, threatening to expose his part in the drug ring unless he killed Darrell Emery. Sorenson planted the car bomb and then Orson took him out so there wouldn't be any witnesses."

"Except us." Rosanna turned to Jess. "We've got our hands on a ticking timebomb. Who do we trust with it?"

"I don't know. Detective Matthews seems pretty solid, but she's Orson's partner. Her loyalty might be to him."

"What about Frye?"

"Maybe. For now, we guard this thing with our lives. Keep laying low."

They decided to watch TV to unwind before going to sleep. "Ten o'clock," Jess said after a sitcom ended. "News time. Let's see what they're saying about us fugitives."

Instead of talking about them the newscaster showed footage of a burning house. "That house looks familiar...oh my God," Rosanna breathed.

"What?"

"That's Lisa's house."

Jess turned up the volume and they listened to the reporter say a gas leak was responsible, causing the explosion while the homeowner, Lisa Woodward, was still inside.

Rosanna grabbed the remote and turned off the TV. "We were just there a few hours ago. What the hell happened?"

"You know what happened," Jess said grimly.

"But how? How did anyone else know about the flashdrive?"

"They must've been watching her," Jess guessed. "They followed her when she went to the bank, saw her get into the safety deposit box, and figured she knew too much."

"This is our fault," Rosanna cried, jumping up from the bed. "We got her involved and now she's dead."

"She was going to get the flashdrive anyway," Jess reminded her. "She said so herself. And she was already involved because she was Darrell Emery's fiancée."

Rosanna began to pace. "When is this going to stop?" she wanted to know. "Cops-who are supposed to be protecting us-are killing people, one by one, who get in their way of cashing in. we saw it firsthand and now someone else is dead, someone innocent. And we're being hunted like animals."

Jess put his hands on her shoulders, stopping her. "We have to keep it together," he told her firmly. "That's the only way we'll get out of this."

"How much more are we supposed to take?" Rosanna demanded. "How much longer can we keep being lucky enough to still be alive?"

Jess just stared at her and she stared back, unblinkingly. Then he pulled her to him and kissed her.

Rosanna was slightly caught off guard but she kissed him back, all the pent-up confusion she was feeling about him finally being released.

The kiss ended and they pulled away, avoiding each other's eyes. "What was that?" Rosanna asked, laughing nervously.

"I think that was a kiss."

"Why did you-"

"I don't know," Jess told her, backing away. "We've been really close together lately…the proximity, the adrenaline…"

"Right." Rosanna nodded. "Close quarters getting to us." She started to walk toward the bed, feeling somewhat disappointed.

Jess sighed. "Wait."

She stopped, turning around. "Yeah?"

"That was a lie," he admitted. "I do know why I kissed you and it's not because of the situation we're in."

"Then why?"

"Because I wanted to," he stated simply.

"In that case, I have a confession to make," she told him. "I wanted you to kiss me."

"So," he said, stepping toward her.

"So," she said back, her heart racing. "Now what?"

Instead of answering, he kissed her again. This time they didn't stop. Jess picked Rosanna up and she wrapped her legs around him, kissing him as they moved, finally falling toward the bed.

Rosanna was sitting up as Jess laid on the bed, pulling her shirt over her head, exposing her smooth skin and black lace bra. Her long dark hair all around her she leaned down, kissing him, one of his hands entwined in her hair.

A while later they were laying in bed, Rosanna's head resting on Jess's chest. "Wow," she said, tracing his forearm with her finger.

"I know," he said back, stroking her hair.

She sat up partway, propping up with her elbow. "I guess all those years of fighting were, what, unresolved sexual tension?"

Jess smiled. "Maybe."

Rosanna sat up farther. "I don't know about you but I think I'm ready for another shower." She got off the bed and held her hand out to him. "Join me?"

Jess took her hand and wordlessly let her lead him to the bathroom.

After they dried off they climbed into bed, their clothes still strewn across the bureau. They laid side by side , staring at the ceiling. "What a night," Rosanna commented.

"I'll second that, Rose." Then Jess stopped, remembering. "I'm sorry. I know you only let Nora call you that."

Rosanna turned his face toward hers with her finger. "It's growing on me."

"Do you regret it?" Jess asked quietly, staring deeply into her eyes.

Rosanna shook her head. "Not a bit."

"Neither do I."

They lay in silence for a while, just staring at one another. Then Jess finally broke it. "For the record, Eric didn't send me to talk to you on his behalf that night," he told her. "I just happened to be in the area, saw you in the store, and decided to press my luck by talking to you about it. I don't like what he did; in fact, I was pretty pissed when he told me. I think your sister's the best thing that ever happened to him, and I didn't want it to really be over. He's my brother, and I want him to be happy." He paused. "But I am sorry your sister was hurt. You're right; she's one of the nicest people I know."

Rosanna stared at him in disbelief. "You really think my sister's the best thing that ever happened to him?"

"Of course I do. Eric's got a great head for business-co-owning one with him was a good career choice after Dad retired-but when it comes to relationships, the man's clueless. He really changed when he met Nora. But I guess not enough," he added regretfully.

"Maybe you were right before," Rosanna said softly. "Maybe he did make a mistake. I don't condone it," she added hurriedly.

Jess pulled her to him and kissed her. "Thanks for that."

"Thanks for what you said." Rosanna kissed him back.

Chapter Ten

"Tom's not in yet so I thought I'd stop by," Elaine told Frye the next morning. "Since it's Saturday he might not come in at all." She shut the door behind her. "But I doubt it."

"Let's see if we can piece all of this together," Frye suggested as Elaine sat down. "When I saw Lisa Woodward yesterday she told me what we already know, that Carolyn Warren was working with and sleeping with Dex Angelo. She made it sound cut and dry, like no one else outside the known drug ring was involved. She also denied that Emery backed up the proof he found, and she was lying."

"Later that day she gets blown up, because of a gas leak," Elaine continued. "After talking to you about Emery and Carolyn Warren."

"Then there's Paul Sorenson, who turned up dead in the river, and all the evidence points to Angelo, who clearly left the country."

"What are you thinking?"

"The M.E. estimated Sorenson's death approximately at nine p.m. Wednesday night," Frye told her.

"Not long after Rosanna Howard and Jess Coleman jumped off the bridge," Elaine said. "Let's say they accidentally witnessed the murder, were discovered, and were running."

"They get cornered in front of the bridge and have no choice but to jump," Frye filled in. "They're too scared to come to us…"

"…because they don't know who to trust," Elaine finished.

Frye nodded. "I told you I suspect Orson's a part of this and now I'm even more convinced." He decided to take the plunge. "I'm fairly certain he was also having an affair with Carolyn Warren."

"How do you-"

"A conversation I overheard between him and Nix a while back," Frye cut in, "who I'm certain is in this up to his neck-"

"We still don't have any solid proof that Tom's involved in this," Elaine pointed out. "It's all theory. Just because he might have been sleeping with Carolyn Warren doesn't mean-"

A knock sounded on the door, interrupting her. Frye called for the person to come in.

Nora Howard entered the room, followed by Eric Frost. "We were told we could find you in here," Nora told Elaine. "We want to know if there are any updates."

"Ms. Howard, Mr. Frost, this is Detective Frye," Elaine told them. "He's consulting with me." She looked at him. "He doesn't think your siblings are fugitives, and neither do I." She turned back to Eric and Nora. "And we're going to try and prove that."

***

Rosanna waited outside the diner while Jess paid, carefully looking around. Then she noticed something a few feet away.

A pay phone.

Rosanna quickly walked toward it, knowing she couldn't take it anymore. She had to call her sister. And it was a pay phone...

She dropped in several coins and shakily dialed her sister's number.

While in Detective Frye's office, Nora's cell phone began to ring. She frowned, not recognizing the number. "Hello?"

"Hey sis," Rosanna said, her voice thick with emotion.

"Rosanna?" Nora asked in disbelief, nodding to Eric. "Where are you?"

"I can't tell you that or much else except I'm okay, and so is Jess." She looked up and saw Jess in front of her. She expected him to be angry but instead he mouthed a message to pass along to his brother. "He's right here and if you see Eric, tell him Jess is okay."

"Eric's with me," Nora told her, looking at Detective Frye, who nodded. "We're at the police station."

Rosanna froze. "The police station?" she repeated in horror. She saw Jess stiffen. "You can't tell them anything, Nora. You can't trust them."

"Why can't I trust them?" Nora asked, eyeing Detective Frye, who motioned for her to give him the phone.

"Ms. Howard? This is Detective Frye," he said into the phone. "Don't hang up," he added hurriedly. "You can trust me."

Rosanna held the phone out slightly so Jess could hear as well. "Why should we trust you?" she asked suspiciously.

"Because I know you and Mr. Coleman are innocent," he told her. "As a show of good faith, I'll tell you something I know."

"What?" Rosanna asked.

"I know Detective Orson was having an affair with Carolyn Warren," Frye told her. "I also know Paul Sorenson was murdered around the time you and Mr. Coleman ended up on the bridge, and the evidence points to someone out of the country." He paused. "I think the two of you saw who really killed Sorenson, and that's why you're running."

"What if we did?" Rosanna asked carefully.

"Then I can help you."

"I still don't know if I can trust you," Rosanna told him.

"And why's that?" Frye asked. "Because the person who killed Sorenson is a cop?"

Rosanna inhaled sharply and looked at Jess, who nodded. "Possibly."

"Ms. Howard, I want to help you and Mr. Coleman. I want you come home safely to your families. If I was part of the coverup I wouldn't be asking for your help, I'd simply come after you. I'm almost certain Tom Orson was part of the drug ring with Carolyn Warren and Dex Angelo. I just don't have any proof. I asked Lisa Woodward yesterday and she denied any existed."

"Lisa Woodward's dead," Rosanna said shortly. "How do we know you didn't kill her?"

"Because I'm saying all of this in front of Detective Matthews, your sister, and Mr. Frost. Also," Frye leaned forward, "if I wanted to kill Lisa Woodward, you, or Mr. Coleman I would've done it yesterday afternoon when you were all together at her house."

Rosanna nearly dropped the phone. "How did you know we were there?" she demanded.

"I didn't believe Ms. Woodward; she was acting suspiciously. So I drove around the block and when I came back I saw you and Mr. Coleman through the window."

"We're supposedly fugitives. Why didn't you arrest us?"

"Because I don't believe you are. I know something scared you enough to make you run, and bringing you in wouldn't be the smartest thing to do right now. I'm not sure who to trust either."

At Jess's urging, Rosanna sighed in resignation. "There is proof," she said, closing her eyes. "Lisa gave it to us. There are names, dates, documents, the works on a flashdrive. It'll tell you everything you want to know."

"Thanks for your trust, Ms. Howard. I promise it's not misplaced. Can we plan a meeting? Get all of this sorted out?"

Rosanna handed the phone to Jess. "How about the pier, off 92nd," he said. "By the telescopes."

"Mr. Coleman," Frye greeted him. "Alright. This afternoon?"

"Two o'clock," Jess said. "Bring Nora's phone so we know it's you."

"Agreed. See you at two." Frye hung up and turned to Nora and Eric. "Everything said in this room stays in this room. Don't talk to anyone other than Detective Matthews or myself."

"They're coming home?" Nora asked.

Frye nodded. "That's the plan."

Jess and Rosanna walked away from the phone. "I'm sorry I broke down and I called her," Rosanna told Jess as they walked. "I couldn't stand it anymore."

"I understand," Jess assured her. "It's a good thing you did. We might finally be getting out of this."

"You're sure we can trust him?"

"He wouldn't have admitted all that stuff in front of more potential witnesses. We already know how badly they want this kept quiet." He took her hand.

"I can't believe it. It's almost over," Rosanna said, squeezing his hand. "We're almost free."

***

Orson sat across from Nix in a coffee shop, casually drinking from his mug. "Thanks for taking care of it so quickly."

"I was lucky to see her coming out of the bank when I did," Nix said. "We know that's where Emery's safe deposit box was..."

"...so now all traces are eliminated. Except Howard and Coleman."

"We're working on it," Nix assured him. "Making it look like they're fugitives was genius. It'll make closing in on them that much easier."

"Good. There have been far too many loose ends to tie up," Orson said. "It's getting sticky." His phone rang. "Orson."

"It's Allison. I went by Frye's office and overheard him on the phone with Howard. She has proof. And Frye, he's onto us, sir. Matthews too. He's meeting Howard and Coleman too."

"Where?"

"I'm not sure."

"Are the brother and sister still there?"

"Walking out the door."

"Grab the sister, meet me on 10th. Tell Ellis to keep an eye on Matthews and Floyd to follow Frye." Orson hung up, shaking his head. "This is getting out of control."

Chapter Eleven

"I feel naked without my phone," Nora said as she followed Eric out the door. "And I wish I could've talked to her longer."

"I know. But it's almost over," Eric told her. "They're coming home." He paused. "I've never been so worried before," he admitted.

"You guys are so close."

Eric nodded. "You and Rosanna too. I know you get it."

Nora nodded her agreement. "I remember when you told me about your mom remarrying," she said, leaning against the railing. "You were four, waiting for your father to come home from San Francisco, but he never did. You told me Frank Coleman was the only father you'd ever known, the only one who ever counted."

Eric smiled. "I was so excited when they had Jess," he remembered. "I always wanted a brother. Half never mattered; he was just my brother." He looked at Nora. "It made no difference."

"I know."

"Anyway, he's coming home. I have to call Mom and Frank. You want to come back with me?"

Nora shook her head. "I need some time to myself. I'll see you this afternoon." She turned to go, then paused. "You've been really great through this."

"So have you."

As Nora headed in the opposite direction to her car, she dropped her keys. When she stood back up a hand clamped tightly over her mouth.

"Don't make a sound," a voice breathed in her ear.

***

Elaine walked out to the back parking lot, deciding to tail Eric and Nora, make sure they weren't followed. As she walked down the back steps, she stopped.

Officer Allison was dragging Nora Howard along at gunpoint.

Elaine drew her weapon and jogged over, pointing the gun at the back of Allison's head. "Drop it!" she ordered him. "Now!"

Allison turned slowly to reveal a terrified Nora Howard. "You don't understand!" he cried, not lowering his gun. "It has to stop."

"Drop the gun, Allison."

"I can't let her go," Allison insisted. "I'll be a dead man."

"That's what you'll be if you don't let her go."

"You drop the gun!" Allison cried, putting his finger on the trigger. "Or I'll shoot her right now!"

A shot rang out then and Elaine froze. Allison began to pitch forward, leaving Nora to jump back in horror.

Elaine saw Tanner a few yards away, his gun still drawn. "Thanks," she told him.

"No problem." He looked at Allison's body. "Why would he take an innocent woman hostage?"

"I think I know," Elaine replied grimly. Then she went to a shaken Nora. "Are you alright?" she asked gently.

Nora nodded. "I guess he was in on it too, huh?"

Elaine turned to Tanner. "Get her to the Captain's office. Get Frost up there too, so everyone's safe."

"What about you?" Tanner asked.

"Frye's going to need backup."

***

"Where the hell is Allison?" Orson muttered, waiting on 10th. Then his phone rang. "Orson."

"It's Ellis. I just saw Matthews stop Allison with the sister. Tanner shot him."

Orson swore out loud. "Where's Matthews now?"

"Going to find Frye." There was a pause. "What do you know."

"What?" Orson demanded.

"I'm on 91st and I see Howard and Coleman, heading to 92nd."

"It's not two yet so they'll be alone. Stop them from meeting Frye. I'm on my way." Orson hung up and got into his car.

"We're early," Rosanna told Jess as they walked up 91st. "Now what?"

"It's crowded; at least we're not too exposed."

"Where's the flashdrive?"

"I've got it," Jess assured her. "Let's get to the pier."

A man bumped into Rosanna, knocking her sideways. "Jess?" she called into the crowd of people.

They were separated.

She saw him a few feet away and was about to call out again when someone grabbed her roughly by the hair, yanking her head back. The grip shifted to her waist and Rosanna tried to fight him off. He spun her around, still grabbing her roughly.

She was looking into the face of Officer Ellis.

"Who has the proof?" he demanded. "You or your boyfriend?"

"Neither of us," Rosanna lied. "We don't trust Frye. I hid it."

"Where?"

"I'll take you to it," Rosanna told him. "If you don't go after Jess."

"Alright. Let's go."

Rosanna turned and elbowed him hard in the gut. "Jess!" she screamed as Ellis doubled over. She broke into a run.

Jess had been looking for Rosanna, then stopped when he heard her scream. He saw her yards away, running from Ellis.

Jess ran after them, his lungs burning from the effort. He saw Ellis grab Rosanna and drag her to his car.

Then he saw the semi hurtling toward it, losing control.

The crowd grew thicker as Jess pushed his way through. The last thing he saw was Ellis opening the car door.

Then he heard the crash.

When Jess got to the sidewalk he saw the semi had crashed into a telephone pole, not before crushing Ellis's police cruiser and knocking it across the street.

As Jess prepared to go to the car it promptly exploded, causing shrieks from the crowd around him. Jess jumped back, horrified.

He looked around frantically to see if they made it out of the car before it was crushed, but no one who looked like Rosanna was anywhere around. Which could only mean one thing.

Rosanna was in the car when the semi hit it. And even if she had somehow survived that, she couldn't have survived the explosion.

His knees giving way, Jess sank to the ground in shock as he realized Rosanna was dead.

**

Orson walked into the abandoned warehouse, followed by Nix and Floyd. They went to the back room, nodding to Ellis in greeting. "Does she have it?"

"She claims she hid it," Ellis told them. "But I don't believe her."

"What now?" Nix asked. "Too many people know about this. We can't kill them all."

"All we need is the backup files. We get that, then we disappear," Orson said.

"How do we get it?" Nix asked.

Orson nodded toward the other side of the room. "Her."

Rosanna was tied to a chair in the back of the room, watching Orson and the others as they spoke in hushed tones. She knew Jess was safe and had theflashdrive; what she didn't know was if he knew she wasn't in the car when it was hit. Ellis had dragged her out of there just in time. Apparently, she was more valuable alive than dead.

For now.

Be okay Jess, she thought as she tried to wiggle out of her ropes. *Please don't do anything stupid.*

Chapter Twelve

Jess walked around listlessly, not even sure where he was going anymore. He could feel the flashdrive in his pocket but that was about it; the rest of him was numb.

He skipped the meeting with Frye, honestly not caring anymore who knew what. He didn't stick around for the fire department or the ambulance; he already knew what he'd hear.

He finally looked up and saw he was in front of a bar. Not caring about laying low any longer, he went inside.

He was the only person sitting at the bar. The bartender looked at him in interest, taking in his worn attire and miserable expression. "What'll it be?"

"Whiskey," Jess told him. "And keep it coming."

The man pulled out a shotglass and filled it with whiskey. "I know that look," he said, sliding the glass over to Jess.

"What look?" Jess asked absently, quickly downing the shot then sliding it back for a refill.

"It's a woman."

Jess drained his glass, staring at the counter. "What makes you say that?"

"I've been doing this for twenty years; I can tell." He filled another glass. "What'd she do? Step out on you? Leave you?"

"You could say that." Jess drank the last drink and threw some bills on the counter. "She's dead."

Jess stumbled out of the bar and into the late afternoon sunlight, squinting. He walked down to the harbor, climbing on top of the railing and sitting with his legs dangling over, staring out into the water.

An image of Rosanna flashed into his mind, from nearly ten years ago. It was freshman orientation day at NYU, and he saw her for the first time yards ahead of him, checking the campus map before walking into the building.

He'd thought she was beautiful.

After that all they did was argue and verbally spar with one another, all four years of college. It got worse when they learned Eric and Nora were dating and catastrophic when they got married. He and Rosanna wasted all their time bickering, instead of really getting to know one another.

But in the past few days, they finally had. Extraordinary circumstances threw them together and they finally let their guards down. And Jess really liked what he saw.

Rosanna had become important to him and now she was gone.

He didn't want to think about what it must have been like for her, how terrified she must have been. What she felt…

What was he going to tell Nora?

Most likely she already knew, given that the cops would've been called and the fact that she was in contact with Frye and Matthews. And Eric…what would he think when he learned Jess hadn't met with Frye?

Jess pulled out the flashdrive, the small data storage device that had caused so much trouble. He was half-tempted to throw it in the water.

But then that would mean Orson and his partners would get away with everything, every death on the list: Carolyn Warren, Darrell Emery, Paul Sorenson, LisaWoodward.

And Rosanna.

As much as he wanted to disappear right now, he couldn't. he had to protect Eric and Nora, and get justice for all those Orson had killed.

His heart heavy, Jess started back down the harbor.

Chapter Thirteen

"I told you, I hid it," Rosanna said through gritted teeth. "It's not here."

"I believe it's not here," Orson said, kneeling down in front of her. "What I don't believe is that you hid it. I think your boyfriend has it."

"No he doesn't," Rosanna said quickly. "I took it from him and I hid it."

"Fine. Where did you hide it?"

"I'm tied to a chair in an abandoned warehouse with four men waiting to kill me as soon as I answer that," Rosanna said edgily. "You really think I'm going to tell you?"

Orson slapped her hard across the face, causing her neck to whip back. Before she could recover he grabbed her roughly by the chin. "You don't want to play with me," he said through clenched teeth. "Tell me where it is."

Rosanna looked hatefully into his eyes. "Go to hell," she snapped venomously.

Orson took out his gun and shoved it against her cheek. "Don't make me ask you again."

"You won't kill me," Rosanna said, trying to keep her voice steady. "You won't take a chance in killing the one person who knows where the flashdrive is."

Orson lowered the gun. "You're right. But I won't lose any sleep sending someone to kill your sister."

Rosanna stiffened. "What?"

"I sent Allison to grab her earlier, wanted to use her as leverage. He screwed it up, though, and got himself killed. That doesn't mean I can't try again."

Rosanna wasn't sure what to do. If she told the truth, they'd go after Jess. If she didn't, they might hurt Nora…

Orson turned to Nix. "Go find the sister."

"Wait!" Rosanna cried out as he turned to go. "Alright." She took a breath. "I didn't hide it anywhere. Jess has it." The words tasted bitter in her mouth, realizing she just made Jess a target. But it was her sister. How was she supposed to make that choice?

"Sold out your boyfriend to protect your sister." Orson chuckled, and Rosanna flinched at his words. "It's clear to see where your loyalties lie." He leaned toward her. "This is what you're going to do. You're going to call the station and ask for Detective Frye. You're not going to say where you are or who has you unless you want me to blow your brains out and go straight after your sister. When you get Frye, ask him if your boyfriend brought in the flashdrive. I'll walk you through the rest…"

***

Jess stumbled into Detective Frye's office, barely able to stand from exhaustion. "Detective Frye?"

Frye looked up at the disheveled young man in his doorway who looked like he needed a hot meal and a solid week of rest. "Can I help you?"

"I'm Jess Coleman." Jess managed to get to Frye's desk and pulled the flashdrive out of his pocket, setting it in front of the detective. "Here's what you wanted."

Frye gestured for him to sit down, concerned he might fall over. He walked over to the coffeemaker and poured a steaming cup, then handed it to Jess. "Get some caffeine in you, warm you up." Frye sat back down. "You missed our meeting."

"I'm sure you can guess why." Jess drank from the cup.

"You couldn't get past that accident with the semi? It was a mess," Frye said. "But that doesn't explain where Ms. Howard is."

Jess blinked. "You know where she is."

"No, I'm afraid I don't. I think I'm missing some of the story here, kid. Why don't you fill me in?"

"Ellis had her," Jess told him, confused. "He was taking her to his car when the semi hit it, crushed it, and then it exploded."

Frye stopped. "You think she was in that car?"

"She had to be. The last thing I saw before the crowd blocked my view was Ellis trying to push her inside."

Frye shook his head. "She wasn't in there."

"What?" Jess demanded.

"CSU checked what was left of the car. It was empty."

Jess nearly spilled his coffee. "Are you telling me she's not dead?"

"I'm telling you she wasn't in that car when it exploded."

Jess felt as though an incredible weight had been lifted; he felt lighter than he had…ever. "I can't believe this," his said, an enormous grin breaking out over his face. "She's alive."

"But she's missing," Frye reminded him. "And you said you last saw her with Ellis?"

Jess nodded, immediately sobering. "Ellis is in on it." He nodded to the flashdrive on Frye's desk. "It's all on there."

"If Ellis has her we have to assume Orson's not far behind," Frye told him. "He hasn't shown his face anywhere near here today, must feel the walls closing in."

"He wants the flashdrive. Ellis grabbed Rosanna because he thought she had it," Jess said slowly. "When he finds out she doesn't…" He trailed off, unable to finish.

"He'll know you have it," Frye said. "He'll use her to get to you." He reached for the phone. "Let me get a hold of Matthews. She escorted your brother and Ms. Howard back to his apartment, where someone's going to patrol to make sure they're protected. She needs to be in on this."

"How is Eric?" Jess wanted to know. "And Nora?"

Before Frye could respond his phone rang. "That's probably Matthews," he told Jess. "Frye," he said into the receiver.

"Detective Frye? It's Rosanna Howard," Rosanna said into the phone Orson held to her lips.

Frye pushed the speaker option on the phone, putting his finger to his lips to tell Jess to stay silent. "Ms. Howard. We've been looking for you."

"Has Jess come by?"

"Yes he has," Frye told her. "Is this about the flashdrive?"

"Did he leave it with you?"

"No he didn't," Frye said steadily, ignoring Jess's surprised expression. "He wanted to wait for you."

"When you talk to him will you tell him I'm at 645 Palmer Street? I'll be waiting for him."

"Anything else?"

"No, that's it," Rosanna replied. Orson took the phone from her and ended the call. "You know he saw right through that," she told him. "He'll probably come with Jess. He might even deliver it himself."

Orson chuckled. "You think I don't know that? It doesn't matter," he informed her. "Once we get what we need, no one's getting out of here."

"You're insane," Rosanna said in disgust. "You're a cop. You're supposed to be upholding the law but you're no better than the people you're supposed to protect us from."

Orson grabbed her roughly by the shoulders. "None of this was supposed to happen," he barked. "I was in it for the extra cash, that's all. Then people had to start running their mouths, threatening to expose me."

"So you became a murderer."

"I did what I had to do. And it would've stopped with Sorenson if you and Coleman hadn't screwed everything to hell. The whole thing's spiraling out of control, and the fallout will be a lot bigger than it had to be." He pushed back from her. "The only thing I know for sure now is I'm getting out before it touches me."

"It already has touched you," Rosanna pointed out. "Proof or no proof, they'll never stop looking for you."

Orson approached her again, only this time he didn't grab her or hit her. Instead he ran his finger down the side of her face, causing her to shudder. "It's always the beautiful ones who get tangled up in these things. First Carolyn, now you." He touched a lock of her dark hair. "Such a waste." He leaned forward to kiss her but Rosanna tilted her head back and spat in his face. "You'll have to kill me first," she snapped contemptuously.

Orson pulled out his gun. "That can be arranged."

"So what happens now?" Jess asked Frye. "Orson has her and wants the flashdrive. What do I do when I take it to him?"

"You're not doing anything alone," Frye told him. "I'm sending you in but I'm bringing backup. Once he thinks he has what he wants, we get Rosanna out of there."

Chapter Fourteen

"Tell me you're not that stupid," Orson said, leaning casually against the wall. "You really expect me to believe you'd come here without the flashdrive and think I'd let her go?"

Jess was in the front room of the warehouse with Orson, who was suspiciously alone. His nerves were shot; all the coffee did was make him feel like he was coming out of his skin. Fighting fatigue and hysteria he stood his ground, saying exactly what Frye told him to say. "I have something you want, you have something I want. I expect an even trade."

"And what about all the cops you brought with you brought with you?" Orson wanted to know. "Like my partner. Or Frye."

"No cops. I'm sure the ones on your payroll already checked," Jess told him. "I want to see Rosanna."

"Fine," Orson relented. "You can see her. Then we talk business." He gestured for Jess to follow him.

They walked through the warehouse to a small room in back that Jess guessed had once been a boiler room. Jess was surprised when Orson unlocked the door and none of his partners were inside.

Rosanna was tied to a chair in the center of the room, looking as tired, dirty, and worn as he felt. There was a large red handprint on her face that made his blood boil.

Relief washed over her expression when she saw him, relief that echoed in him. "Are you okay?" he asked, surprised by the emotion in his voice.

She nodded. "I'm fine."

"See? Out of her own mouth," Orson said. "Now. Enough stalling. Where's the flashdrive?"

"Let her go first."

"Mr. Coleman, you're really trying my patience." Orson walked over to Rosanna and drew his gun aiming it at her temple. Her face immediately drained of color. "Don't make me ask you again."

Frye, where are you? Jess thought in a panic. He'd stalled long enough for the reinforcements to arrive. What was holding them up?

"Now, Mr. Coleman. I don't know how much longer I can control my finger here." He nodded toward the trigger.

"Alright!" Jess cried. "Alright. It's at the next building over, in the metal trash bin out front."

Orson continued to hold his gun on Rosanna. "So you picked the girl over your own safety. Too bad she didn't do the same for you."

"What are you talking about?"

"I gave her a choice earlier," Orson explain as Rosanna began to cry silently, tears sliding down her face. "Protect you or herself-"

"No!" Rosanna cried, crying in earnest. "It was Nora, Jess. He said he'd kill Nora."

"It's okay, baby," he told her sincerely. "She's your sister. I understand-"

Before Jess could continue Orson lowered his gun, stepping away from Rosanna. In one swift stroke he pistol-whipped Jess in the back of the head.

Jess fell to the ground, dizzy and disoriented as Rosanna cried out. He could see Orson's blurry shape walk to the door, pausing by the gas outlet. "You've both been in my way too damned long." With the blunt of his gun he knocked off the valve; a hissing sound filled the room. "Now that's over." He left the room, locking the metal door behind him.

"Jess? Can you hear me? Are you okay?"

Jess rolled onto his back, looking up at the fuzzy ceiling. Though images were overlapping he could tell the room was windowless and airtight. He began to cough.

Rosanna was working on her ropes, still struggling to get free. Jess dragged himself over to her, attempting to help. "It's okay," she told him. "I've almost got it." At last she undid the final knot, shoving the ropes aside. She immediately dropped to the floor, cradling Jess's head in her lap. "Hell of a reunion, huh?" he asked, managing a small laugh. Rosanna smiled despite herself. "Airport reunions have nothing on us." Her nose wrinkled involuntarily. "It's really strong."

"Frye's coming," Jess informed her. "He had it all set up. He'll catch Orson on his way to the empty trash bin. Frye already checked the flashdrive, verified the evidence. He's here to arrest them all."

"He better hurry," Rosanna said, coughing lightly. "It's coming in fast." She looked down at Jess. "Look at you," she murmured, brushing the hair off his forehead. "What you went through to get to me."

"You have no idea." He looked up at her soberly. "I thought you were dead."

"I'm sorry," Rosanna said sincerely. "Ellis grabbed me and I tried to fight him off…we got out of the car just in time. Then he dragged me off." She paused. "You thought I didn't get out?"

Jess nodded. "The car was smashed, then it exploded…I couldn't believe it. I went all around town, not caring who saw me or if someone found me. I was really messed up."

"You were?" Rosanna whispered.

"Of course I was." He touched her hair. "I never got to tell you that I don't hate you."

"I don't hate you either," she said quietly. "It would've been hell going through this alone," she told him and he raised an eyebrow. "I'm not saying it's been a picnic," she said, smiling wryly as she looked around. "But you know what I mean."

"I do. And I feel the same way."

Outside at the next building over, Orson kicked the empty metal trash bin, cursing out loud. He should've known the kid was lying; it was a rookie mistake.

His desperation was making him sloppy.

"Freeze!" he heard a voice yell from behind him.

Orson slowly turned around to see Matthews a few feet away, her weapon drawn and aimed at him. He shook his head slowly. "You don't want to do that."

"Hands in the air, Tom."

"I don't know what you think you know," he began, "but it's all a lie. A frame-up. I can explain-"

"There's nothing to explain. We've got the flashdrive. You, Nix, Ellis, and Floyd are all going down for this." She took a step closer. "Don't make this harder than it has to be."

"You've got it wrong, Elaine," he said softly. "Come on. You know me."

"No one knows you, Tom. You had everyone fooled. Me most of all." Her voice cracked. "How could you do it?"

Instead of answering he pulled out his own weapon, aiming it at her. They stood there, standing off. "I don't want to shoot you," he told her honestly. "You've been a good partner, and a good friend. Just let me get out of here, tell them I got the drop on you. No one will ever know."

"I'll know," she said quietly. "I can't let you get away with all you've done. You have to be held accountable."

Orson shook his head regretfully. "I'm sorry Elaine."

Floyd appeared from behind her, tackling her to the ground. As Orson started to run someone materialized from the shadows, blocking his path.

"Don't bother looking for Ellis and Nix," Frye told him, moving forward. "They're in custody. And you're joining them."

"Like hell." Orson charged Frye.

Elaine got the upper hand with Floyd, pinning him to the ground. "Where are Howard and Coleman?" she demanded.

Floyd glared up at her. "Go to hell."

Elaine jabbed her gun in his throat. "No one will ever believe it wasn't provoked. Tell me," she ordered.

"The back," Floyd managed. "The boiler room."

Elaine took his gun and cuffed him to the pole nearby. Then she went to assist Frye.

Frye was on the ground, Orson choking him. Frye struggled for his gun, on the ground a few feet away. Orson applied more pressure.

A shot rang out.

Frye was aware of the pressure on his throat being alleviated. His eyes focused on Orson, on the bright red stain seeping through his shirt. His eyes widening, Orson dropped to the ground beside Frye.

"You okay?"

Frye nodded, slowly sitting up. Elaine had moved over to Orson's body next to him, kneeling down. "You were doing your job," Frye told her, rising to his feet.

Elaine nodded, standing. "I know. But he was still my partner." She turned to Frye. "Floyd said they're in the boiler room. Backup's on the way, along with EMS." She started for the building, Frye following.

They got into the back, to the old iron door. "This must be it," Frye said, feeling for the latch. "It's stuck."

Elaine helped him, applying force to the old, rusted latch. It finally gave way, and the door opened.

Elaine and Frye immediately stepped back, coughing. "Gas," she muttered. "We have to get them out of here."

They went inside, blocking their mouths and noses with their arms. Rosanna was slumped forward across Jess's stomach, who was flat of the ground.

Elaine grabbed Rosanna and dragged her out the door, Frye following with Jess. "I hear sirens," Elaine said as they laid them on the ground. She turned to Rosanna. "Rosanna? Can you hear me?" Frye acted identically, trying to revive Jess. Neither of them stirred.

"They're both breathing," Frye said. "They just need to hold on a little longer."

EMS workers came in then with stretchers, and Elaine and Frye followed them as they wheeled Rosanna and Jess out. "I'll ride with them," Elaine told Frye. "Call their families."

Frye nodded. "I'll meet you there."

Jess and Rosanna were wheeled through the E.R., Elaine left behind. She leaned up against the wall, closing her eyes in exhaustion.

Frye arrived shortly after, approaching her. "Hell of a gash you got there," he said, pointing above her right eyebrow.

"Floyd caught me by surprise. Are the family members on the way?"

Frye nodded. "You should let someone look at that. I'll let you know when I hear anything."

"Frost and Howard?"

"I'll take care of it."

Elaine nodded, then slowly made her way down the hall.

Frye made his way to the waiting room, knowing Frost and Howard would want their questions answered when they arrived. He sank into a chair, feeling incredibly drained.

Shortly after sitting he heard scrambling footsteps. Looking up he saw Eric Frost and Nora Howard rapidly approaching him. "Where are they?" Nora demanded. "Are they alright?"

"They're in the E.R.," Frye answered. "We'll be notified as soon as there's news."

"What happened?" Eric wanted to know. "Why are they here?"

"They were trapped in a boiler room with a gas leak," Frye told them. "They're being treated for inhaling the fumes."

"How bad is it?" Nora asked quietly. "The truth."

"I'm no doctor," Frye told her, "but …I hope we got there in time. They were unconscious when we found them."

Jess and Rosanna were side by side in a cubicle, being worked on. The first thing Jess was aware of was the oxygen mask, the bright lights, blurring images, and jumbled sounds.

He was vaguely aware of someone saying "he's awake" and all the frantic movement around him. His head rolled to the side as the images started to focus and he saw someone laying a foot away from him.

Rosanna.

Doctors were working on her but she wasn't stirring. She too had an oxygen mask but continued to remain motionless.

Jess could feel that his lungs were working, could tell he was starting to breathe more easily. Reaching out with his arm, he tried to grab Rosanna's hand.

With his free hand he pushed the oxygen mask away, despite the doctor and nurses' protests. "Rosanna," he said weakly, brushing his hand against hers. "Don't do this to me again." His mask was put back on but he continued to touch her hand.

And felt her brush his hand back.

Jess smiled as her eyelids fluttered and her head turned to the side. Her eyes were focused on his.

Feeling relieved Jess stopped fighting the nurses and let them wheel him out of the room.

Chapter Fifteen

Elaine looked up as the door opened, nodding to Frye as he walked into the room. "Couple stitches," she said, looking upward. "Nurse is coming back with the paperwork."

"Not too bad," he said, leaning against the closed door. "They're going to be fine," he informed her. "Their families are with them right now."

"Good. Now this nightmare can be over."

"Pretty much. Ellis, Nix, and Floyd have all been charged. With the evidence we have it should be open-and-shut." He looked at her. "How are you doing?"

"Fine."

"Really? Because if I just found out the partner I trusted and worked with for a year had been involved in a drug ring, murdered four people, and I had to be the one to stop him from doing more…I wouldn't be fine."

Elaine shrugged. "You caught me. I'm not fine. The truth is, I don't know what the hell to be. I don't know how I'm supposed to keep doing this job when the bad guys turn out to be some of our own."

"It's tough," Frye told her. "No matter how long we're in this we still get surprised by new lows. It's a lot to take." He pushed away from the door. "Normally, I prefer to work alone because, frankly, there's not too many people I work well with." He opened the door. "You're one of the few I don't mind having around."

Elaine managed a small smile. "You're not so bad to work with either."

***

"Ms. Howard? I need a few moments to check her vitals."

Nora blinked, slowly rising from the uncomfortable plastic chair she'd been glued to for the past few hours, watching her sister sleep. The doctor said Rosanna would make a full recovery but she needed a lot of rest to recover from all her body had been through. Even though Nora knew she'd be okay, she hadn't left her bedside.

But now the nurse was forcing her to, so she had no choice. She walked down the hall to the vending machines and called their parents to let them know everything was fine and that she'd meet them at the airport tomorrow when they arrived from Florida.

After she made the call she got a bottle of water from the machine and began to drink, walking listlessly down the hall. When she passed room 310 she stopped, looking through the window.

Eric was sitting at Jess's bedside, just as she had been sitting at Rosanna's. Only Jess was awake, listening to whatever his brother was saying and managing a laugh. Taking a breath, Nora ventured in.

""Sorry if I'm interrupting," she began as she stepped inside. "I just wanted to see how Jess was doing."

"You're not interrupting," Jess told her from his bed. "Come in. Sit."

Eric immediately vacated his chair so she could sit down, and she nodded her thanks.

"How's Rosanna?" Jess asked immediately.

"Fine," she told him. "Sleeping. She's been in and out for the past few hours and I'm just around while she gets her rest."

"That's what I'm trying to get this one to do," Eric began, "but he hasn't been cooperating."

"I've been sleeping some," Jess protested. "Anyway, I like the company."

Nora looked at him for a moment. "I'm glad you're alright," she told him finally. "I know we're not technically related anymore but you were my brother-in-law for five years and…I thought of you as a brother. I still do." She paused. "I also know what you did, going after Rosanna like that. You took a hell of a risk, and you almost died. Both of you did." She swallowed hard, then squeezed his hand. "Thank you."

"You're welcome," he told her. "And, for what it's worth, I still think of you as a sister too."

"It's worth a lot," Nora said, blinking back tears. "I need to get back. Are your parents flying in?"

"I just got off the phone with Mom," Eric spoke up. "She and Frank should be getting in tomorrow afternoon."

"Good." She leaned over, kissing Jess on the forehead. "Get some rest. I'll see you soon." She nodded to Eric on her way out.

"Why are you still here?" Jess asked after she shut the door. "Go after her."

Eric nodded. "I'll be right back."

Nora was halfway down the hall to Rosanna's room when she heard her name being called. She turned to see Eric jogging toward her. "What's up?" she asked, surprised.

"Thanks for checking on Jess," he told her. "He always thought a lot of you."

"The feeling's mutual." She paused, feeling awkward. "Is that all?"

"No." He took a breath. "I'm sorry," he told her sincerely. "For everything."

"You've already apologized-"

"I know. There's more." He looked at her carefully. "All this time I've been telling you how sorry I am, trying to win you back. I was being selfish, only thinking about what I wanted, how much I needed to have you back. But that's not what you need."

Nora didn't know what to say.

"Ever since we found out Jess and Rosanna were missing, all I could think about was family. It made me really see what I did to ours and asking you to get past that was too much. I won't do it anymore."

"What are you saying?" Nora asked softly.

"I'm saying I'm letting you go, respecting the fact that we're divorced now. I won't push you into forgiving me anymore. I'm giving you the space you deserved all along."

Nora was crying freely now. "You've been so supportive these past few days," she choked out. "And now this…" She went to him, wrapping him in a hug. "I'm sorry, too. And I'm sorry it's over." She pulled back. "And I've already forgiven you."

"Can we stop fighting now? It might make it easier, seeing as how my brother and your sister have become friends. Maybe even more than that."

Nora nodded. "Who could've seen that coming?" She looked at him. "No more fighting."

"Good. Now…" he trailed off.

"Now we start over somehow," she told him. "Try to move on." She looked down the hall. "We both need to get back."

Eric nodded. "Take care of yourself," he told her.

"I will. You do the same."

He watched her walk away until she disappeared into her sister's room. Then he turned around and started in the opposite direction.

"Well?" Jess asked when he returned. "How did it go?"

"Good," he told his brother, sitting down. "We're going our separate ways without bloodshed, wished each other well. Now," he said, leaning forward, "I want to talk about you."

"What about me?"

"First of all, I want to say if you ever scare the hell out of me like that again kid, I'll kill you," Eric said sternly, his tone etched with concern.

"Got it. The second thing?"

"What the hell's going on with you and Rosanna? For years you've hated each other, then you get caught up together in the real-life equivalent of an action movie, and now…what? You're into each other?"

"It's a long story," Jess told him. "But since we have the time…"

***

Rosanna opened her eyes Sunday morning to bright sunlight streaking through the window, slotted from the blinds. It was the first time since she arrived at the hospital that she really felt awake.

And hungry.

"Morning, sunshine."

Rosanna blinked, focusing on her sister. "You're still here? You should've gone home, gotten some sleep."

"I'll get all the sleep I want tonight. You're being released this afternoon, and you're coming home with me."

"That's not really necessary," Rosanna said. "I'll be fine."

"Sure you will. Mom and Dad will be there too."

"What?"

"I'm going to pick them up from the airport soon. Face it, sis. The next few days are family time."

"Great." Secretly, Rosanna didn't mind. "I'm starving. Is there any way I can get a real breakfast?"

"Not a problem." Nora stood. "I need to stretch my legs." She paused. "When I get back we need to have a serious talk."

"About what?"

"What really happened between you and Jess."

"Nora-"

"You put me through hell, worrying me the way you did. You owe me some girl talk." She shouldered her purse. "Besides…maybe I think it's a good thing."

"You do?"

Nora nodded. "Believe it or not, I think you're good for each other."

A knock sounded on the door. "Come in," Rosanna called.

The door opened and in came Jess in a wheelchair, pushed by a nurse who promptly left after warning him not to stay too long. "How's it going?"

"I can't believe you're out of bed. Where's your brother?"

"He picked up Mom and Dad from the airport and took them to a hotel to get settled in," Jess replied. "So I thought I'd come and say hi."

"I see you're in good hands," Nora said. "I'll get plenty of food so Jess can eat too." She left.

Jess wheeled himself closer to Rosanna's bed. "They're springing me this afternoon," he told her brightly.

"Me too. Nora insists on taking me home with her. Mom and Dad are coming too." She paused. "How are you?"

"Surprisingly good. I could use some more sleep and I never want to walk anywhere again, but other than that I'm alright. You?"

"Tired," Rosanna admitted. "I'm in no rush to get back to work anytime soon." She paused again. "Grateful that we're sitting here talking to each other."

"There's a lot to talk about."

"I know. Where do you want to start?"

He looked at her. "What's going on with us?" he asked softly.

"I don't know," she said honestly. "It's definitely new territory."

"It is."

"How do we know what's real?" she asked quietly. "We were thrown into an intense situation, fighting for our lives...maybe the chaos is what brought us together."

"It might've brought us together but I don't think it stops there. At least not for me," Jess told her. "Thinking you were dead, seeing you in the E.R. before you woke up...it doesn't get more real than that. Three times is too damned much, Rose."

"I know." She reached for his hand. "When we were in that boiler room and I thought we wouldn't make it out...all I thought about was all the time we wasted fighting. I don't want to waste it anymore."

"Neither do I." He squeezed her hand. "What would you say if I asked you out on a date?"

"I wouldn't know what to think without someone shooting at us, almost drowning, or almost dying from gas poisoning. What will we do for fun?"

Jess grinned. "Something completely boring."

"Sounds good to me."

Epilogue

One Week Later

The sun was starting to sink over the horizon, casting the city in a golden red glow. There might have been noise and bustle from the crowded city streets but out in the cemetery it was quiet, peaceful.

Dex Angelo stood with a bouquet of roses in front of a grave, reading the gleaming headstone:

Carolyn Ann Warren
1973-2008

As he knelt down the last night he saw her flashed across his mind. They were arguing at first, as usual, but then it turned into more. Despite the business they were in, the fact that she was married, or the fact that she had someone else on the side, Dex loved her in his own way. It made him sick every night to think that he trusted Tom Orson, that he couldn't have seen the signs sooner. But it was too late to be sorry now.

Dex carefully laid down the roses and stood, blinking in the sunlight. For a moment he thought he heard Carolyn laughing, sounding happier than he'd ever heard her before. Then he shook his head sadly and left the cemetery.

***

"Thanks for signing your statements," Elaine told Jess and Rosanna. "We won't be seeing you again until the trial." She shook both their hands. "Good luck to you both."

"Thanks for all your help," Jess told her and Detective Frye.

"Thank you," Frye told them. "You'd both make hell of detectives."

Jess and Rosanna exchanged a glance. "I think we'll pass," Rosanna said with a wink. Then they left.

"That wraps that up," Elaine said, walking back to her desk.

"Not quite." Frye walked over to her. "I talked to the Captain. He seems to think I need a partner."

"Yeah?"

"What do you think? Want to give it a shot?" He stuck out his hand.

Elaine considered for a moment. "Only if we agree to stay out of each other's way."

"Deal." They shook on it.

Jess and Rosanna walked out into the cool night air, hand in hand. "So," Jess asked as they walked to the parking lot, "ready for our first date?"

Rosanna nodded. "It's a great choice too. A nice, quiet evening watching movies at my apartment. No drama, no excitement, no wrong turns in an alley."

"I don't know," Jess said, leaning up against his car, pulling her to him. "I'm up for a *little* excitement."

"What do you have in mind?" Rosanna asked playfully.

"Up for a shower?" Jess wiggled his eyebrows.

"Always." Rosanna kissed him.

THE END

Made in the USA
Columbia, SC
08 December 2022

72999569R00048